. Nolan's
s.

Co-authored by William F. Nolan

LOGAN'S RUN

and published by Corgi Books

Wonderworlds

William F. Nolan

CORGI BOOKS
A DIVISION OF TRANSWORLD PUBLISHERS LTD

WONDERWORLDS

A CORGI BOOK 0 552 11081 7

First published in Great Britain by Victor Gollancz Ltd

PRINTING HISTORY

Gollancz edition published 1977
Corgi edition published 1979

To the memory of ERNEST MILLER HEMINGWAY who never wrote a word of science fiction—and who would be surprised to find several of his selves in this book.

This book is set in Linotype Pilgrim

Corgi Books are published by Transworld Publishers Ltd.,
Century House, 61–63 Uxbridge Road, Ealing, London, W5 5SA

Made and printed in Great Britain by
Richard Clay (The Chaucer Press), Ltd., Bungay, Suffolk.

CONTENTS

AUTHOR'S PREFACE

The twenty-one stories in this book span more than two full decades—from the 1950s into the 1970s—representing a prime involvement in the fields of fantasy and science fiction. During these two decades I have been involved in every possible aspect of the sf genre: as an artist, fanzine editor, amateur publisher, convention organizer, book and magazine editor, lecturer, book reviewer, script writer in films for TV, novelist and, as this collection demonstrates, short story writer.

All the stories in this book have been published in the United States, but the majority have never appeared in England. Several of them, despite their fictional plot lines, contain autobiographical elements. Example: 'Kelly, Fredric Michael: 1928–1987.' My mother's maiden name was Kelly; my father was named Michael. He died of cancer in a California hospital under the exact conditions described. Many other 'bits' in this story are based on memories of my Missouri childhood: reading Mickey Mouse, watching Gary Cooper and the Lone Ranger at Saturday matinees, sledding in winter, fishing with Dad at the Lake of the Ozarks, reading the dog stories of James Oliver Curwood ... and I, too, was born in 1928.

I transferred my Missouri background to Kansas in writing 'But I Have Promises to Keep ...' and the lead character's remembered emotions are my own; Robert Murdock's strong parental love is quite real—and my favourite boyhood pal, Jack Morgan, appears here as a character under his real name. (And Jack, where are you now?) The poem by Robert Frost inspired this story, but my awe of deep space and of the men who will one day travel out to the stars shaped its plot.

My first important fiction sale was made to *Playboy* magazine early in 1956, and was a major factor in my decision to quit office work and become a full-time writer. As a freelancer, *Playboy* became one of my best markets, and I placed a variety of pieces with the magazine over the years following that initial sale. Among these was 'Papa's Planet', which grew out of my knowledge of Hemingway's world, plus my fascination with android robots. 'Papa's Planet' practically wrote itself.

Other stories were far more difficult; in fact, the creative root system of 'Starblood' is frustratingly complex.

It began not as a short story, but as portions of several novels. Three of the sections, 'Tris', 'Morgan', and 'Bax', were originally the first chapters of three science fiction novels that died aborning. I had not been able (or willing) to pursue the plots further. Yet I *liked* these opening segments, and filed them away. Finally, I placed an overall frame around them, involving my version of the 'aliens-invading-Earth' concept, revised them to fit this frame and added three new sections. Result: 'Starblood', a story I was honoured to have selected for a 'year's best' science fiction anthology.

In line with fictional root systems, all writers are asked the inevitable question: 'Where do you get your ideas?' Of course, there is no single answer, since story ideas spring from a wide variety of sources—including dreams.

'He Kilt It With a Stick', my study of a cat-killer, came to me in a dream. The entire desperate situation in which my character finds himself occurred, full-blown, in my nightmare. I awoke cold and shaking. Later, in a calmer mood, I put my dream to paper.

Another tale in this collection stems directly from the nightmare of a stranger ...

I was in New York on business, staying at a hotel in the heart of the city. It was late, and I was asleep—when a man's voice woke me. Muted, filtered through the wall of my hotel room, repeating a phrase over and over in an agonized tone: 'I've killed ... I've killed ... I've killed.'

I was about to call the desk when the voice stopped—and did not resume. By morning, the room was empty. For years I wondered about the tortured individual on the other side of that wall. *Who was he?* I gave myself an answer by writing 'Coincidence'.

I'm a cinema addict. I see at least two motion pictures a week, and have done so since I was old enough to totter down the aisle of a movie palace. I moved to Los Angeles in 1953, and immediately began exploring the Hollywood film industry. I visited the studios, made friends with producers, directors, actors—and, as a natural consequence, have written many screenplays and television scripts. Not all of them sold. 'Operation Gorf', my nutty tale about a giant frog, began life as a misguided screenplay in the late 1950s. It never jelled, and was buried in my files. Much later, I got out the 'Gorf' folder and realized that this unsold script had in it the makings of a wonderfully looney short story. Thus, my giant frog was finally launched.

One of the most stimulating afternoons of my life was spent with James Bond's creator, Ian Fleming—in November of 1959. I was an avid Fleming buff when we met that day in Chicago, and owned mint British editions of all his Bond thrillers. We spent a marvellous afternoon together touring the famed shootout sites of the Capone era for a travel book Fleming was writing—and I found the man to be as fascinating as his fiction.

'Fasterfaster!' is my parody-tribute to Fleming, updated as science fiction. I like to think it would have amused him. At least I had a great deal of fun writing it.

And that's the key to this whole business for me: *fun*. Writing fantastic fiction is a constant delight, a method of entertaining others as I entertain myself.

That's my job—to entertain—and the wonderworlds of science fiction and fantasy collected in this volume represent a full cross-section of my imagination: a mix of light and heavy, bright and dark. I had fun putting them all on paper. I trust you'll share that fun in reading them.

William F. Nolan
Los Angeles, California
1976

KELLY, FREDRIC MICHAEL: 1928–1987

MONITORED THOUGHT PATTERNS CONTINUE:

... wrong, twisted ... and I'm being ... being ... Steen is already ... they want me to free-form again ... goddamn it. I don't understand just what this ...

We had a coal-burning furnace with a slotted iron door in the basement, and you broke up the clinkers inside with a poker, lifting the door latch with the heat sweating you ...

... and Mickey left Minnie standing at the little white picket fence. She was blushing. 'Love ya,' he said. 'Gee,' she said. 'Gotta fly the mail for Uncle Sam,' he said. 'Golly, you're so brave!' she said. His plane was a cute single-seater, with a smiling face and rubbery wings ...

The Moon! They'd made it after all, by God, and Armstrong was walking, jiggling, kind of floating sometimes, with sixty million or more of us watching. He could still be a part of it. He was only forty-one and that wasn't old—not too old if he really ...

... kept shooting, but the bullets bounced right off his chest. 'Time someone taught you fellows a lesson in manners!' He tucked a thug under each arm, pin-striped suits with hats still on, and leaped through the window of the skyscraper, him in the air now and them yelling and him smiling, square-jawed, with that little black curl over his forehead and the red cape flaring out behind, soaring above the poorly drawn city with the two ...

... alone in the back of the car, the two of them, not watching the movie (a comedy with Hope in drag and Benny pretending to be his daughter), not giving a damn about the movie. 'Don't, Freddie. I can't let you.' Sure she could. He'd taken her out often enough for her to let him.

He wouldn't hurt her, ever. He was sure he loved her—or if he didn't, he *would*, if she'd just ... '... never have come here with you if I thought you'd—' His hand touched her soft thigh, and she was ...

... tight against the rocks with the Arabs coming. The legion guy next to Coop was plenty nervous. 'Think we can hold 'em off?' And Coop smiled that slow, easy, boy-smile that meant nothing could touch him; we all knew nothing could touch Coop. 'Sure. Sure we can. They won't attack at night. We'll slip out after dark.' He fired twice and two fanatic Arabs fell, in close-up. A hidden ground wire tripped their horses, but we were too young to know about hidden ground wires ...

'... so I'm going to tell Dawson he can go to hell!' 'They'll bounce you right out,' I told Bob. 'So what. So who needs a Ph.D. from this lousy ... Look, man, I don't *need* college. Dawson is a phony, lying bastard, and he knows it. And so do his students, but they just sit there listening to him spout out his ...'

... planet wants me to ... no, no ... it isn't the planet itself. It isn't alive, doesn't tell me anything ... dead planet out here on the fringe of the System ... but it has ... a kind of influence, in conjunction with the rest of this System ... the whole thing is a form of ... new force, or ... damn it, I wish they'd let me ... just wouldn't ...

Mother wanted to know what I was doing in my bedroom all alone for so long and I said reading a Big-Little-Book and she came in to see. I had a pretty fair collection, and the best were the ones set on the planet Mongo. 'You read too much. It'll ruin your eyes.' She was smiling and roughing my hair, which I hated, but I didn't hate her. I loved her, very, very much. '... to sleep now. You can read more tomorrow.' The room was small and comfortable and I could smell her perfume and the special soap she used and I liked the way she smiled, always ...

... rowing close to the shore, along the rocks, while he

fed line into the quiet lake. 'This is where the fat ones like to come in,' Dad said. The sky was so blue it hurt my eyes, so I kept my head down. A mosquito bit me. That was the only trouble with lakes, the mosquitos. They loved water the way Dad did. I liked rowing, feeling the long wooden boat slide through the water with Dad feeding out his line, and the lake black-green with no motorboats on it, quiet and hot and ...

... I kept thinking what JoAnn's father would say if he knew. He always worried about JoAnn. 'You two kids take care, ya hear?' And then he'd say, 'I trust you, Fred, because you're a Catholic.' And I assured him that I'd never ...

... more ... keep wanting more ... I'm being ... forced to spill out all the ...

'Hey, Kelly, the old man wants to see you.' Sure he did, and I knew why. Because I was late three mornings this week. I had reasons. The lousy freeways were jammed, so I took surface streets—but Old Harker would never listen to reason. 'Tell him I won't be late anymore.' I was going to the Moon. To work there. To train for space. And someday, with luck, maybe I could ...

Wow! Pie right in the kisser. The little tramp wipes it off, sucks his thumb, does a kind of ballet step back, and falls down three flights of stairs. Terrific! Up he bounces, dusts the seat of his baggy pants, tips his hat, spins his cane, and walks into a cop! WHOMP! Cop is furious. Jumps up and down, shaking his stick. The tramp does a polite little bow, tips his hat again, and ducks between the cop's legs. ZING—right down the middle of the street. Cars missing them by inches. Two more cops join the first cop. Three more. A dozen. Falling and yelling. Tramp is up a fire escape, over a roof, through a fat lady's apartment—she's in the tub!—out a door, down an alley, and then the ...

... snow came and I'd rush for the basement to dig out my old sled. Rust had coated the runners with a thin red film and I had to get them shiny again with sandpaper, doing it fast, wanting to get out on the hill and cut loose. School closed, the hill waiting, Tommy Griffith yelling at me to get a move on, and then the long whooshing slide down from Troost with snowdust in your nose and steering to miss Tommy's sled and picking up speed coming on to Forest, mittens and yellow snow goggles and the warm coat Uncle Frank got you for Christmas . . .

. . . while his father was *dying*. The hall smelled of white paint and starch and, faintly, of urine. Hospital smells. The young priest had been emotionless about it, kept smiling at him and saying 'A passel of years' when he told him how old his father was. He was glad to be out of Holy Mother Church, because she didn't really give a damn about him or his father. He hoped God did, somewhere, but not Holy Mother Church. What did it matter how old his father was? So what? He was still dying of cancer and you never want to go that way, no matter *how* old you are, even if . . .

'My country 'tis of thee,
Sweet land of liberty . . .'

Sing it, boy—sing it loud, and let the world know that you're an American. Sure he was too young to fight, but he was proud. And scared, too. They were giving us hell on those beaches. Giving us bloody hell . . .

. . . born in 1928 . . . into space when I was fifty. Moon first, then Mars . . . If I could just tell them straight, and they didn't . . . keep trying to force all the . . . it's 1987 and I'm fifty-nine years old and I shouldn't even be on this planet . . . said I was too old, but nobody listened. Experience. We need you out there, Fred. Help chart the new Systems. Warps did it, made it all possible . . . one jump, and into another galaxy. No dream. Fact. Cold reality. All right, then, I volunteered . . . but not for this . . . didn't know I'd ever be . . . goddamn sick of being . . . sucked dry this way . . . without my having any choice in how I . . .

*

'That's it! Oh, that's fine! Keep coming, honey!' Mom, with her arms out. Wobble. Almost into the lamp. 'C'mon, son, you can do it. *Walk* to me!' Daddy there, kneeling next to her, looking excited. The room swaying. Terror. Falling. Rug in my face. Sneezing, with them laughing and pulling me up and me trying again, better this time. Steady now, and Daddy was ...

... feeding her power, letting her drift out, then snapping her back. 'You're great, Fred,' Anne told me. 'Nope. Car's great,' I said. 'Handles, doesn't she? Richie did the suspension. Short throw on the shift. Four downdraft carbs. She'll do 200 easy. And a road like this, she eats it up.' Life was good. Power under my foot and power in my mind and the future waiting ...

'... when the sniper got him.' 'What?' 'Sniper. In Dealy Plaza.' 'Where's that?' 'Texas.' 'What was he doing there?' 'Wife was with him. They were—' 'She dead too?' 'No, just him. Blood all over her dress, but she's fine. She's fine ...'

'... so let's see what he looks like under that mask.' Oh, oh, they *had* him now. Guns on him, his hands tied, no chance to get away. 'Yeah, Jake, let's us have a good look at him.' SPAAAAANG! 'What the—' Oh, boy, just in time. Neat! 'It's the durn Injun! Near killed me. Looks like he's got us boxed in.' What are they going to do? 'Better untie me, Jake, and I'll see to it that you both get a fair trial in Carson City.' Deep, strong voice. No other voice like his! 'You have my word on it.' They won't. Or *will* they? Not much choice. SPAAAANG! 'His next shot won't miss, Jake.' Oh, they're scared now, all right. Look at them sweat. 'Guess we'd better do as the masked man says,' the big one growls. SPAAAANG! Boy, if they don't ...

'... go to Mars! Fred, you know we can't go to Mars!' I wanted to know why not. 'Because, for one thing, Bobby is too settled in. His school, all his friends, everything is here. The Moon is his *home*.' I told her I was going, that it was a job opportunity I couldn't afford to miss. But she kept up the argument, kept ...

... on his stomach under the porch with the James Oliver Curwood book, the one about the dog who runs away and falls in love with a wolf and they have a son who's half dog and half wolf. He'd found it in the basement when he was ten. It was his favourite James Oliver Curwood. Rain outside, making cat-paw sounds on the porch, but he was dry and secret underneath, all the good reading ahead. He pushed a jawbreaker, one of the red ones, into his mouth and ...

'... let her go! Dammit, Fred, she doesn't want to hear from you. She's never going to answer you. She wants to forget you.' That was all right. Sue was still his wife and they still had their son and maybe he could put it all back together. He'd visit them on Bobby's birthday, and maybe he could ...

The stars ... the *stars* ... a massed hive of spacefire, a swarm of constellations ... the diamonds of God ... It was worth it—worth everything to be out here, a part of *this*. Everything else was ...

... enough! I've given enough ... sick ... exhausted ... hollow inside, drained ... pulped out ... They were lucky, the others were lucky and didn't know it, dying with the ship ... but they took us down here, two of us ... and Steen's insane now ... They got ... He free-formed until they ... I know ... know what they still want from me, what they have to experience along with all the rest of it ... before they're satisfied. They want to taste that too—the final thing ... Well, give it to them. Why not? There's no way back to anywhere ... Your friends are gone ... Steen's a raving fool ... so give them the final thing they want, goddamn them ... whoever they are ... whatever they are ... Just give them ...

THOUGHT PATTERN ENDS.

PAIRUPS, INC.

When Thirdburt turned twenty-one, his father threw him bodily out of the family lifeunit in New Connecticut.

'Why is this happening?' Thirdburt wanted to know.

'Firstburt is mate-paired, and so is Secondburt,' father Bigburt said. 'You are now twenty-one and it is time for you to be mate-paired. Frankly, your mother and I are worried about your sexual thrust.'

'My sexual thrust is A-oke. Perfectly A-oke,' said Thirdburt. 'I just don't fancy the idea of being rushed into pair-mating when I'm not one hundred per cent emotionally receptive to a full snugdown situation.'

'Son,' said Bigburt, 'my terms are simple: unless you've acquired a state-approved pairmate within twenty-four hours, I'll disinherit you. Throwing you bodily out of our lifeunit was harsh, but necessary. Your mother and I must make certain you are a par-socio norm and not some kind of sub-socio misfit.'

Thirdburt shook artificial yard pebbles from his hair. 'So what do you suggest, Dad?'

'I suggest you apply down at Pairups, Inc. They'll computermate you jiffdandy for a nominal fee.'

'But I don't have a nominal fee.'

Bigburt handed him 400 creds. 'This ought to do it,' he said.

And he slammed the lifeunit's door in his son's face.

PAIRUPS, INC, the glowsign blinked. Below, other glow-letters formed the company motto: 'The Love of Your Life for the Life of Your Love.'

Thirdburt walked briskly through the slidentry and confronted the receptclerk, a distinguished mid-aged female robot.

'Love solves all,' she said to him. 'Wars never solved anything. Hate never solved anything. Love is a bracing tonic, a rainbow in a clouded sky. Love is a dappled horse in a meadow of—'

'How much?' asked Thirdburt.

'Sir?'

'For a pairmate selection. How much?'

The robot sniffed. 'Three hundred eighty-six creds, including your state-required honeymoon.'

'Can't I arrange my own honeymoon?'

'Not since Pairmate Law 26-G took effect last month,' said the robot. 'Whether or not you allow a pairmate selection centre to choose your bride your honeymoon *must* be computerized.'

'Well, what if I don't want to go on one?'

The robot clucked. 'Pairmates are required to honeymoon. It's a socio-norm.'

Thirdburt shrugged his thin shoulders. 'Oke. Guess I'll take the package.' He handed the clerk 386 creds.

'Please follow Cupid's Arrow,' she said, slotting the money.

'To where?'

'Don't ask useless questions,' the clerk snapped. 'Useless questions overincrease my voltage receptors and I'm liable to malfunction.'

'I guess I spooked you when I cut in on your telling me that love was a dappled horse.'

'I like to finish what I start,' admitted the robot.

'Accept my apologies,' said Thirdburt. 'But I'm on a tight schedule.'

And he began to follow a wide, glowing arrow which shone up through the nearglass flooring. The arrow led him down a long metallic hallway to a musical slidedoor marked PAIRMATE SELECTION DATA. With a flourish of wedding chimes, the door slid open and Thirdburt walked through.

Facing him was a floor-to-ceiling wall of spinning discs and blinking multicoloured lights.

'I'm Harvey, your friendly datacomputer wall,' the wall said to Thirdburt. 'My job is simple. You tell me everything about yourself and I select the ideal pairmate for you. Are we ready?'

Thirdburt nodded.

'You'll have to speak up,' the wall declared. 'Nodding or head-shaking is not going to get us anywhere.'

'Can I sit down?'

'That isn't allowed at this point,' said the wall. 'Let's begin with age, height, weight, colour of eyes, waist and neck dimensions, chest girth, length of limbs, blood type, and family birth data. Rightie?'

'Rightie,' said Thirdburt. He gave the wall its requested data, then said, 'This is all pretty boring.'

'Not to me, it isn't,' said the computer wall. 'I eat up stuff like this. For example, I can get very excited over a man's chest girth.'

'That's an odd thing to admit,' said Thirdburt.

The wall giggled, then got serious again. 'Now, then,' it said. 'I need some really intimate data. And don't be shy.'

'What kind of data?'

'I can't pairmate you precisely if I don't have lots of intimate stuff to go on. Like ... tell me about your most disgusting sex-thrust dreams.'

'I don't have any.'

Several of the wall's little lights wavered. 'But that's impossible! Everyone has disgusting sex-thrust dreams.'

'Not me,' said Thirdburt firmly. 'I'm a very sound sleeper. In fact, father Bigburt was forced to wake me from a very sound and satisfying sleep in order to throw me bodily out of our lifeunit this morning.'

'Tush,' said the wall, readjusting its lights. Some of the rapidly spinning discs stopped spinning, while others started to spin. 'You're making it tough for me.'

'Sorry,' said Thirdburt, scuffing one shoe against the near-glass flooring.

'Now,' said the wall in a patient tone, 'just what are you looking for in a pairmate?'

'I'm not looking for anything,' declared Thirdburt. 'This is all father Bigburt's idea.'

'Let me put the question another way. In past sex-thrust

situations, what elements have attracted you?'

'I'm a virgin,' said Thirdburt, 'so I wouldn't know.'

'Gad!' exclaimed the wall. 'You are the first twenty-one-year-old male sex-thrust virgin I've dealt with in a coon's age!'

'What is a coon's age?'

'It's an ancient expression dealing with the lifespan of a long-extinct animal. Forget I ever said it.'

'All right, but I'm basically curious about things like that.'

'We're way off the track,' said the wall, with a trace of metallic irritation.

'Then ask me something.'

'Food,' said the wall. 'What's your favourite food?'

'Fried breadplant with nearfruit topping, cooked in banana oil and served from an open platter garnished with sweetpeas,' said Thirdburt.

'I wish I could eat stuff like that,' sighed the wall. Then it asked, 'Favourite hobby?'

'Skeeterhopping.'

'With or without a skeeter?'

'Without.'

'How would you sum up your personal philosophy?'

'I'm really not very philosophical,' admitted Thirdburt, 'I just kind of drift along from day to day, lacking a driving force to better my condition.'

'You're not a very colourful person, are you?' asked the wall.

'Not very. I see myself as a kind of puce yellow.'

'Have you ever experienced instant rage? Ever wanted to maim or rape?'

'Not that I can recall,' said Thirdburt. 'I'd be likely to remember something like that, wouldn't I?'

'I'd say so,' the wall remarked.

'I wish I could make things easier for you,' said Thirdburt. 'But, frankly, I wouldn't even be here if my ole Dad hadn't threatened to disinherit me.'

'Then you really have no strong central desire to be pair-mated?'

'I can take it or leave it. I'm not anti, if that's what you're getting at. It's just that I'm not very pro.'

'I've handled toughies before,' stated the wall. 'I have over ten trillion electronic neurons inside me working for you at this very moment.'

'That's a lot of neurons,' said Thirdburt.

'I was hoping for something really *intimate* from you. I thrive on intimacy.'

'I trust you won't be offended,' said Thirdburt, 'but I find you a rather odd computer wall.'

'Really?' said the wall. 'Odd is a word I might well apply to you. Life isn't all breadplant with nearfruit topping, cooked in banana oil, you know.'

'Served from an open platter garnished with sweetpeas,' added Thirdburt. 'Can I leave now? I've given you plenty of data to process. So process it.'

'Don't tell me my job,' snapped the wall.

'It's just that I'm getting tired of standing here talking to a wall,' said Thirdburt. 'I really am.'

'Follow Cupid's Arrow to the Loveroom and wait there,' the wall told him. 'I'll send in your pairmate.'

'How long will it take?'

'Just follow the arrow,' said the computer wall. 'Our interview is concluded.'

And the musical slidedoor opened as the glowing arrow appeared.

Thirdburt shrugged and left the chamber.

In the heart-shaped Loveroom, Thirdburt sat down on a heart-shaped lovechair. The chair sighed.

The room was soft and warm. The walls were pink and fuzzy, and so was the robot who rolled over to Thirdburt.

'Excited?' asked the robot.

'Not particularly,' said Thirdburt.

'Bet you can't wait for the honeymoon to start?'

'I'd like to get it over with.'

The robot rolled completely around the chair, talking as it rolled. 'Your honeymoon is my baby. Just leave everything to me. You are in capable hands.'

'I'm glad to know that,' said Thirdburt. 'In all truth, your datacomputer wall is a little wacko.'

'Oh, Harry's all right, once you get used to him,' said the pink machine. 'He's just sensation-hungry.'

'He told me his name was Harvey.'

'Harry or Harvey, what real difference does it make?'

'Seems to me you machines would know each other.'

The fuzzy robot tipped on two wheels as it rolled across the floor, quickly righting itself. 'I roll too fast and I get into trouble that way,' it said. 'What were we talking about?'

'Names,' said Thirdburt.

'Call me Albert. That'll suit me fine.'

'When does my pairmate get here?'

'Soon. Ought to be soon now. Excited, huh?'

'I said not very. What I am is impatient.'

'What kind of girl did you ask for?' The machine rolled crazily around a heart-shaped lamp, one of its little wheels bumping over the base.

'I left all that up to the wall,' said Thirdburt.

'Well, it's not vitally important. What's vitally important is your honeymoon. That's what we should be concerned about. That's where our attentionspan should be concentrated. There's nothing I like better than putting through a good, solid, state-approved honeymoon for two young people in love.'

'Love has nothing to do with this,' said Thirdburt.

'Love makes my wheels go round,' said the machine named Albert.

'I'm glad you're happy in your work,' said Thirdburt, biting a knuckle. He was getting restless.

The lovechair sighed under him.

'Why does my chair keep sighing?'

'All part of the atmosphere here at Pairups,' said the rolling robot. 'We had a pillow that used to croon Gypsy love songs until they took it out. It got too erotic. We watch that. Thin line. Save the hot stuff for later.'

'I'm thirsty,' said Thirdburt.

'No problem.' The fuzzy machine rolled over to a tall silver dispense-all, filled a cup, and rolled back with it.

Thirdburt said thanks and drank the liquid. Then he handed back the cup. 'Tastes funny,' he said.

'Made from rose petals,' said the robot. 'Needs more sugar. I keep telling 'em that up front, but they won't listen to me.'

'I'm really getting impatient,' said Thirdburt.

'Why not lie down on our lovecouch with a thick, comfy lovepillow under your head? Would you like to do that?'

'No, I wouldn't.'

The machine rolled into a table, knocking a heart-shaped vase of nearflowers to the floor. The vase shattered.

'You're getting me nervous,' said the machine. 'I'm knocking things over.'

'Then stop rolling around,' advised Thirdburt.

'Hey, here's your pairmate!' A tiny green light blinked on the robot's fuzzy chest. 'Now we can both relax.'

A plump, bearded man with red-rimmed eyes stepped into the Loveroom. He wore flarewaist riding knickers, a flow-checked vest and a long-billed baseball cap—and he looked confused.

'There's been an obvious mistake,' said Thirdburt. 'That's not my pairmate. He's not even female.'

The fuzzy robot clucked, 'I'm sorry the choice is not entirely to your satisfaction, but we must proceed as scheduled once the pairmate selection has been completed.'

'But it *hasn't* been,' Thirdburt objected. 'This bearded fatty is totally unacceptable as a pairmate. Totally.'

The rotund man in the long-billed baseball cap shook his head slowly. 'I don't get any of this dingo you're passing out. I came here to repair the lousy atomic furnace. Instead, I end up in this keeky heart-shaped room with a dumb-looking fuzzy pink robot and a bug-faced creep who calls me fatty. I'm not fat, I'm *beefy*.'

'Same thing,' muttered Thirdburt.

'Not so,' declared the man. 'There's a whole world of difference between being fat and being beefy.'

'If you're here to repair an atomic furnace,' said Thirdburt, 'then why are you wearing flarewaist riding knickers, a flowchecked vest and a long-billed baseball cap?'

'Because I'm odd,' said the big man defensively. 'And odd people always wear odd clothing. I'm a Genuine Oddity. That's my state right, you know!'

'I know, I know,' said Thirdburt. 'I simply found it curious.'

'Allow me to point out,' said the pink machine, 'that we at Pairups, Inc. stand ready to sever, legally, under state-approved separation laws—and for a nominal fee—a malfunctioning pairmate relationship such as yours. Post-honeymoon, of course.'

'Honeymoon?' boomed the bearded man. 'What's this fuzzy dingo talking about?'

'I'd best explain all this, clearly and concisely,' said Thirdburt. 'You'd better sit down.'

The beefy repairman settled into a love chair. It sighed deeply. 'Damn thing's alive!'

'It's programmed to sigh,' said Thirdburt.

The fuzzy pink robot rolled nervously around the room, tiny wheels crunching shards of broken vase. It was muttering to itself.

'My name is Thirdburt. I came in here to be pairmated so my father wouldn't disinherit me. After extensive questioning relative to my choice of a pairmate, a computer wall named Harvey, or Harry, selected *you* as my pairmate. An obvious error that cannot, at this point, be rectified. This agitated pink robot is here to arrange our state-approved honeymoon, and I see no recourse other than to go on with it. Later, we'll take Albert up on his separation offer. That's his name, Albert.'

'And what if I don't play along with this drek?' asked the bearded man. 'What if I just lay you two dingos out cold and split loose?'

'Oh no, no, no,' piped the rolling robot. 'You must believe me when I tell you that we have ways of dealing with violence. If you attempt any form of threatening physical action, you will be rendered senseless and will be sent on your honeymoon in this unfortunate condition.'

'He means it,' said Thirdburt.

The bearded man glared at them both, then slumped back in the chair. 'I just hope they get somebody to fix the lousy furnace,' he said.

'Now, then,' began the robot. A blue disc began rotating in its head. 'Name, sir? I need it for my data spool.'

'Felix One,' said the atomic repairman.

'Fine,' said the robot. He rolled around the chair to face the two pairmates. 'Now, folks, as to the *type* of honeymoon, we have a pleasantly wide selection. There are Lunar sightseeing honeymoons, romantic jetboat excursion honeymoons, rugged fishing and hunting honeymoons, Martian sandcraft excur—'

'The one you just said,' cut in Thirdburt. 'The rugged fishing and hunting one.' He swung towards Felix. 'Is that one oke with you?'

'Sure,' the big man nodded numbly. 'It's your shindig.'

'Can we camp under the stars near a large body of water?' asked Thirdburt. 'I've always wanted to do that.'

'Certainly,' replied the fuzzy machine. 'All of our fishing-hunting honeymoons come automatically equipped with a large body of water.'

Thirdburt bit his lower lip thoughtfully. 'You know,' he said, 'this might work out after all.'

Felix One grunted.

'Hi, kids, I'm your jolly roadroller,' said the square, red-wheeled machine to Thirdburt and Felix as they stood outside the main building at Pairups, Inc. 'You two cuddle-cuties hop aboard and we're on our fun-filled way to a memorable state-approved honeymoon in a preselected, wildly primitive, totally sterile wilderness.'

'How can it be both?' Thirdburt wanted to know.

'Both what?'

'Both wildly primitive and totally sterile.'

'Let's not delay our departure with nonfunctional over-verbalization. Your answer is inherent in the trip itself.

Now, in with you two lovedoves, it's time to roll.'

'Cut the lovedove, cuddlecutie drek,' snapped Felix.

The square machine ignored him and began to move out.

'That's the way he's programmed,' said Thirdburt. 'We'll just have to accept this sort of thing.'

At jato speeds, the roadroller whipped them deep into wilderness country, humming along narrow roads cut through thick, green forest.

'What kind of trees are those?' asked Thirdburt.

'Nearoak and nearpine and nearspruce,' said the rolling machine. 'And there are a few nearcottonwoods. They all have real pseudoleafmould under them. We at Pairups, Inc. take justifiable pride in our expertly simulated natural environment. No cheap plastic stuff for us. We don't jack around when it comes to quality.'

'I see,' nodded Thirdburt.

Felix grunted.

As the sun was setting behind the trees in splendid style, they arrived at their primitive campsite on the banks of a roaring river.

'How do you like the place?' the square machine asked Thirdburt.

'Looks oke to me,' he said.

'All of your fishing-hunting gear is stowed in your good-natured lovetent,' the roadroller said.

On the shore, a few dozen feet ahead of them, a large, fuzzy pink tent suddenly popped up.

'The tent, as you have just seen, is self-inflating. When you wish to move, just ask it to deflate and follow you. Now I'm going to tippy-toe away and leave you two kids alone.'

The car sniggered and rolled softly away into the dusk.

'Hey!' yelled Felix, running after it. He shook his head, turning back to Thirdburt. 'Is the damn thing just going to roll off and *abandon* us out here?'

'I'm sure he'll be back for us at some preselected time,' said Thirdburt.

'Hi, pairmates. I'm your adaptable, good-natured pop-up

lovetent, patent pending,' said the tent as they approached it.

Thirdburt said hello.

'I know that both of you must be a wee bit concerned about my overseeing your, as it were, intimate moments,' said the tent.

'What moments?' Felix asked.

'I refer to your pash periods.'

'We're not having any,' growled Felix. 'The dingo data-computer wall screwed up. I'm really an atomic furnace repairman, and this gink is—'

'As I was saying,' the tent continued, 'when you cuddle-bugs want privacy for those special pairmate snuggle sessions ... well, there's a little pink hickey on my centre peg. Just press it and switch me off. Otherwise, I'm apt to be intrusive.'

'He didn't listen,' complained Felix.

'I told you,' said Thirdburt. 'They're all programmed to treat us like love-starved pairmates. Accept it. Won't hurt you any.'

'Makes me feel creepy,' said Felix.

'Might I now prepare a rustic wilderness repast for the two of you?' asked the tent.'

'Sure, go ahead,' said Thirdburt.

'First, you must get into your Zippies,' said the tent. 'All honeymooners must wear Zippies while honeymooning. State law 47-J. Duck under my flap and you'll find them.'

Thirdburt and Felix ducked under the fuzzy flap. Two fuzzy pink-zippered jumpsuits were laid out for them on a double lovecot.

'Do we have to put on these dingo outfits?' asked Felix.

'You heard him. State law,' said Thirdburt, neatly zippering himself into his Zippie.

'Right, right,' snarled Felix, zippering furiously. 'But I like to select my own odd clothing.'

The tent snickered at this remark and Felix slapped a fist against the centre peg's pink hickey. 'There, you fuzzy bastard!'

'You'll just have to activate him again,' said Thirdburt.

'He can't fix our meal if he's switched off.'

'You do it.'

Thirdburt activated the tent.

'Why don't you two lovedoves wait outside?' suggested the tent. 'I'll sing out when the chow's on.'

Thirdburt and Felix sat down on the soft bank of the river, watching the water roar fiercely over large black boulders.

'Looks rough out there,' said Felix.

'We can adjust it,' said Thirdburt. 'This plastocard says so. I found it in the tent.'

Felix read the card.

> NOTICE: If you find the river is too severe in action, you may reduce it according to personal preference. Use the projecting knob on the piece of neardriftwood on the shore to adjust the river's flow. Thank you.
>
> Pairups, Inc.

'I'm going to try it,' said Thirdburt.

He walked over to the piece of neardriftwood, located the knob and twisted. Instantly, the roaring torrent became a gentle flow. 'Works,' said Thirdburt.

Felix nodded. He looked morose. 'Adjustable rivers depress me,' he said.

The tent yelled at them, 'Chow's on!'

They ducked under the fuzzy flap and sat down at a long table. Platters of food popped up from the table's interior.

'Hey, boy!' exclaimed Thirdburt. 'It's fried breadplant with nearfruit topping, cooked in banana oil and served from an open platter garnished with sweetpeas!'

'I can't eat that bilge,' Felix told the tent.

'Oh, yes you can,' said the tent.

'What do you mean, "Oh, yes I can?"'

'I mean you eat what I lay out. *I'm* the chef. I decide what to serve.'

Felix grabbed a fishing pole and a pair of hip-length boots and stormed out of the tent. 'I'll catch my own dinner!'

The tent snickered.

Outside, Felix pulled on the boots and, wading out into mid-river, cast his line. Within ten minutes, he'd caught three fat trout and five silver lake bass. He carried these into the tent and slapped them on the table.

Thirdburt did not look up; he was fully occupied with his fried breadplant.

'There!' said Felix. 'What say to that?'

'I say,' said the tent, 'that you have caught several fat, delicious-looking nearfish.'

'You mean I can't eat 'em?'

'Not unless you are equipped to digest electronic circuitry,' said the tent.

Felix tossed aside the pole and slumped on to the nearoak bench next to Thirdburt. 'Pass the breadplant,' he said dully.

The tent clucked in satisfaction.

Deep night. The pneumobed rocked and soothed them, but what annoyed Felix, in particular, was what the bed kept whispering.

'Cut out the lousy erotic suggestions,' snapped Felix as the bed raised itself on one side, nudging him towards Thirdburt.

'I was simply attempting to get you into a pash-period mood,' declared the bed.

'Well, we just want to sleep,' said Felix.

'Some honeymoon!' remarked the bed sourly.

Thirdburt, by now, was snoring—which kept Felix awake for another hour. When he drifted off, he had a nightmare about being swallowed by an atomic furnace.

'Chow time!' the tent announced.

It was light outside; the morning sun had just cleared the tips of the neartrees. Robot birds were twittering sweetly.

'I need rest,' said Felix. Thirdburt was already up.

'Nonsense,' said the tent. 'There's a lot to do. You have to hunt today.'

'That's right,' said the bed, dumping Felix on to the floor.

'We'd best do as the tent says,' Thirdburt advised, helping the bearded repairman to his feet.

'Into your Zippie,' said the tent. 'Then you eat and hunt.'

'Fun,' said the bed.

After a breakfast of fried breadplant on nub toast, they left the tent, hunting gear strapped to their backs, rifles in hand.

'What are we supposed to hunt?' asked Felix.

'I have a list,' said Thirdburt, staring at a sheet of near-paper. 'The tent said we can have our choice.'

'What's on the list?'

'Neargeese, automated wild rhino, and electroelephants,' said Thirdburt.

'You name it.'

'I've always had a kind of yen to hunt big game,' said Thirdburt. 'Let's go after the automated wild rhino.'

'Where are they?' Felix shifted the hunting gear strapped to his back. 'I hope we don't have to walk much farther.'

'Jungle Trail No. 3,' said Thirdburt. 'We follow that into the "artfully simulated rhino country." It's all here on the list.'

'Then let's get going. My back is killing me. Repairing atomic furnaces just doesn't give you the muscles for this sort of drek.'

They located the proper trail and followed it into deep pseudobrush, which eventually opened into rolling hill country, studded with clumps of high grass.

'I guess we're here,' said Thirdburt, shading his eyes to peer about.

'There's a water hole,' said Felix, pointing. 'From what I read once, rhinos seem to favour water holes.'

'Oke. Let's stake out there.'

They tramped over to the water hole. Thirdburt nodded towards the mud. 'Rhino tracks,' he said.

Felix grunted, seating himself on a large grey boulder. He eased the pack from his shoulders, put aside his rifle.

'The list says the rhino is a "fast and treacherous beast"

and to watch out for his horn,' said Thirdburt.

'You kill one, I'll just sit here,' said Felix.

'You know, I'm really beginning to enjoy our honeymoon,' Thirdburt observed. The brush rattled behind him.

'Look out!' shouted the bearded atomic repairman. 'Here comes a really big one.'

A two-ton horned rhino galloped straight at Thirdburt, head lowered for the kill.

'You take him,' said Thirdburt, handing Felix his rifle.

'No, sir, *you* take him.' He tossed back the weapon. 'And you better not miss. He's almost on top of us.'

'I just wanted you to have the fun of downing the first one,' said Thirdburt. 'I'm not selfish.'

'Shoot! Shoot!'

Thirdburt sighted along the barrel at the charging beast and pressed the trigger.

Two nearslugs slammed into the head of the galloping rhino. He faltered, eyes rolling, and dropped at Thirdburt's feet.

As the two hunters leaned close to him, he winked. 'Got me!' said the rhino. 'My heartfelt congratulations on a perfect kill! Next, I'm sure you'll want to try the electro-elephants. They're even meaner than I am.'

The rhino got up, shook trail dust from his leathery hide, and nodded with his horn. 'Just follow jungle trail No. 6 to the left. You can't miss 'em.'

And he trotted away into the high grass.

'That wasn't as much fun as I thought it would be,' said Thirdburt. 'I think if he hadn't *talked* to us, I would have liked it better. Let's tackle the elephants.'

Along jungle trail No. 6, the trees began to shake. Sparks jumped from their trunks.

'What the deuce is happening to those dingo trees?' Felix asked.

'I think the jungle is shorting out,' said Thirdburt. 'Some kind of electrical problem. We'd better get—'

One of the sparking trees erupted into smoke and fell directly on Felix.

Thirdburt pushed aside nearleaves and pseudobranches to reach the fallen atomic furnace repairman.

'Are you all right, Felix?'

'It got me,' moaned the bearded man. 'It really nailed me. I'm done for.'

'What exactly do you mean?'

'I mean that this damned electrical tree has killed me,' said Felix.

And his head rolled loosely.

'Is he gone?'

Thirdburt peered through the trees at a pale figure crouched in leaf shadows.

'Who are you?' he asked. 'Are you some kind of electronic ape?'

'Of course not,' said the shadowy figure. 'I'm as human as you are. What I want to know is—is he gone?'

'Gone where?'

'Is he *dead*?'

'Oh. Yes, I'm sure he is.'

'Good!' The pale figure emerged from the trees and Thirdburt gasped.

'What's the matter with you? Haven't you ever seen a beautiful nude girl before?'

'As a matter of fact, I haven't. I'm still a virgin.'

The girl who was blonde and full-bodied, knelt beside Felix and checked his pulse. 'He's gone, sure enough.' She raised an eyebrow at Thirdburt. 'What are you doing out here in the jungle with this bearded fatty?'

'A computer wall selected him as my pairmate by mistake,' he told the blonde. 'I'm a victim of malfunction.'

'Me too,' said the girl. 'That's why I'm out here, nude in the nearwoods.'

'For my sake, I'm glad,' Thirdburt admitted. 'I really admire your melony breasts.'

'Yes, they are nice,' agreed the blonde. 'I come from a chesty family. My name is Firstlinda. What's yours?'

'Thirdburt.'

They shook hands.

'If this fatty hadn't died out here, I'd still be in trouble. Now everything's jimdandy.'

'I don't understand,' Thirdburt said, staring at her ripe thighs.

'I came out here on the regular pairmate honeymoon set-up,' the nude girl explained. 'But my pairmate was a pseudo-animal freak who ditched me for a rhino. He took this rhino back with him as his pairmate and left me here with no food or clothing.'

'What happened to your Zippie?'

'He put it on the rhino so the lovetent wouldn't get wise to a switch. Out here clothes make the man—or the rhino, as the case may be.' She giggled and her pink tummy, which was lightly dusted with golden hair, quivered.

'That's some tummy you have,' Thirdburt remarked. 'And your pubic area is nice, too.'

She smiled at him. 'You *like* me, don't you?'

'Sure, a lot. Your being nude and beautiful helps. If you were fully clothed and ugly, I *might* still like you—but it's doubtful.'

'I appreciate directness in a man,' she said, stripping the Zippie from Felix One.

'Why are you doing that?'

'I thought I'd made it clear to you,' said the girl. 'The tent won't accept me as your pairmate unless I'm wearing a Zippie.'

'I see.'

'These machines don't actually differentiate between male and female. According to an electroelephant who witnessed the whole thing, when my pairmate brought the rhino back to camp, the tent accepted the pair of them. And when he put my street dress on the rhino, the roadroller picked them up without a hitch and returned them to civilization. I couldn't get picked up because I was mateless. Now, thanks to that tree falling on the fatty, I have *you*.'

'What still puzzles me,' said Thirdburt, 'is what your

original pairmate wanted with an automated rhino.'

'I told you. He's a pseudoanimal freak. The wall messed up in pairing us. I'd never honeymoon with a pseudoanimal freak if I knew he was one in advance.'

'Makes sense,' nodded Thirdburt.

'Well . . . how do I look?'

The girl was fully clothed in Felix One's pink Zippie.

'I liked you better nude,' said Thirdburt.

It was late when they arrived back in camp. The tent greeted them cheerfully.

'Bet you're both starved.'

'We'd rather cuddle first,' said the girl. She smiled at Thirdburt.

'Certainly. Your lovecot is all prepared.'

They ducked under the flap.

'Happy cuddling,' the tent said.

The girl pinched Thirdburt's left buttock. 'Hope you don't mind if I take advantage of the situation?'

'Not at all,' he said, and, trembling, switched off the tent.

By morning he was far from virginal.

'Well, I see you have a legally-stamped, state-approved pairmate honeymoon certificate,' said Bigburt to his son when Thirdburt returned to the family lifeunit.

'That's right, Dad.'

'And where's your pairmate?'

'Died on the honeymoon,' said Thirdburt.

'Terrible. A terrible tragedy.'

'Yes, Dad, that describes it perfectly.'

'How did it happen?'

'The jungle shorted out and a tree fell over.'

'Terrible.'

'May I assume that I have regained your parental approval and that I am not to be disinherited?'

Bigburt patted his son on the head. 'The family fortune is yours to share.'

'Thanks,' said Thirdburt.

All in all, mishaps considered, Thirdburt felt that he had been on a very satisfactory honeymoon.

But it was good to be home again.

STARBLOOD

Is the orbit stabilized?

Yes.

How much longer to penetration?

Soon now.

You first. Then I'll follow.

Do you think ... I mean, is it possible, with this planet, that we'll be able to succeed?

We'll try. That's all we can do. I have no answers.

1
Bobby

Bobby was still crying, his tiny face red, fists clenched, ignoring the roboMother who rocked and crooned to him.

Dennison walked over, switching off the machine, and picked up his son. He carried the squalling infant to the patio where his wife was playing Magneball with an android instructor.

'Bobby's been crying all afternoon,' Dennison said. 'Do something with him. See if you can't shut him up.'

Mrs. Dennison glared at her husband. 'Let Mother handle him.'

'I switched her off,' said Dennison. 'She wasn't doing any good. Take him for a ride in the copter. He likes that. It'll shut him up.'

'You do it,' said Alice Dennison. 'I'm perfecting my back thrust. I play tournament next week, you know.'

'You don't give a damn about your son, do you?'

She nodded to the android, ignoring the question. 'Ready,' she said.

A magnetic disc leaped from the instructor's hand and the woman expertly repelled it with a thrusting left glove.

'Well done, Mrs Dennison,' said the android.

In a silent rage, Dennison advanced on the android and beheaded the machine with a metal cane.

'I hope you're satisfied,' said the wife. 'They cost fifteen thousand dollars. I'll just have to buy another.'

'You do that,' said Dennison. 'But first you take Bobby up in the copter. I can't stand any more of his squalling.'

She scooped up the baby, who continued to howl, and took a riser to the roofpad. Activating the family flier, she placed Bobby inside and lifted off in a whir of gleaming blades.

Five miles above New Chicago Mrs. Dennison switched the copter to autoflight, unlatched the main exit panel and held her baby son straight out into the blast of air.

She smiled at him—and released her grip.

Still crying, Bobby Dennison fell twisting and tumbling towards the cold earth below.

2
Tris

In Greater New York, under warm summer sun, the walkways sang. Heat from the sky stirred delicate filaments within the moving bands and a thin silver rain of music drifted up to the walkriders, soothing them, easing away some small bit of city hive pressure.

For Tris, an ex-Saint at sixteen, the pressures were mounting and the song of the walkways did not ease her; she was close to an emotional breakpoint. When a Saint is cast out by the Gods she has nowhere to go. Society shuns the outcast. Her only chance lies in reinstating herself. If she cannot achieve this, she ceases to function as a viable entity and self-extinction is her only recourse.

Tris was beautiful and free-spirited, with a body built for

Sainthood. Surely, she told herself, she would find her way back into Divine Favour.

'The Reader will see you now,' said the wallspeak. 'Inside and just to the left.'

Tris moved ahead past the sliding wall and turned left.

Reader Sterning was ready for her, a tall man in flow-silks. His smile was warmly professional. They touched palms and Tris sat down.

'Well, well,' said Sterning. 'I can surface why you're here, and believe me when I tell you that I sympathize.'

'Thank you, Reader,' said the girl softly.

'How long were you a Saint?'

Tris knitted her fingers in her lap, twisting her hands nervously. She'd never been deeped before and it was a little frightening. 'Could you . . . turn off the wall?' she asked.

'Of course,' smiled Sterning, and killed the hypnowall. The swirl of colours faded to black. 'I really don't need it in your case. I want you to be as comfortable as possible. Now . . .' He tented his hands. 'How long were you a Saint?'

She blinked rapidly. 'For almost a year. One of the Gods selected me in Omaha. They were there to flare and I offered . . .'

'You offered your Eternal Self?'

'Yes, that's right. And they accepted me. One of them did, I mean.'

'The one called Denbo, am I correct?'

She nodded, flushing. 'He took me. He sainted me.'

Sterning bowed his head. 'A rare sexual honour. A beautiful selection. And you *are*. Quite.'

Tris blinked again. 'Quite?'

'Quite beautiful. Thighs . . . hips . . . breasts. You are ideally qualified for Sainthood.' He sighed. 'Your situation is most unfortunate. But let's get to it.'

He moved around the desk, sat down close to her on the flowcouch, his dark eyes probing. 'Lean back and relax. I'm going to deep you now. Close your eyes.'

Tris shuddered; she knew there would be no pain, but the *nakedness* of it all! Her inner mind laid bare to another!

'You needn't be concerned about opening to me,' Sterning said. 'It's all quite normal. Deeping is a natural process for those of us who read. You have nothing to be afraid of.'

'I know that,' said Tris. 'But . . . it isn't easy for me.'

'Relax . . . just relax.'

She settled back into the chair, her mind opening to his.

Sterning shifted to a below-surface level, sighed. 'Ah, sadness and guilt.' He began reading. 'You were a truly passionate Saint and the Gods were pleased. And you got on well with the other Saints, sharing their life and dedication until . . .'

He hesitated, probing deeper. 'Until you made a mistake which cost you Divine Favour.'

'Yes,' murmured Tris. Her down-closed lashes quivered against her white cheek. 'A mistake. I should never have—'

'—criticized.' Sterning finished the thought. 'You criticized a God and they banished you. Your comments were cruel, caustic.'

'I was angry,' said Tris. 'With Denbo.'

'Because he was sexually favouring other Saints.'

'Yes.'

'But you had no right to be angry. A God may bestow his sexual favours where he will. That is his Divine right, is it not?'

'I know, I know,' said the girl. 'But I thought Denbo—'

'—would consider your feelings. But of course no God need consider a Saint's feelings. That is your mortal flaw. You cannot accept nor abide by Divine rule.'

'I *tried* to obey, to accept.' The girl was beginning to cry, her eyes still closed. Tears ran down her cheeks.

Sterning continued to probe, unmoved by emotion. 'You failed out of sheer stubborn self-pride. You felt . . .' He moved to a deeper level. 'You felt equal to Denbo, equal to a God. You desired more than Sainthood.'

'Yes.' Softly.

'And what do you want from me?'

'An answer. Surely, within my brain, somewhere within it, you can read a way back.'

The Reader stood up, breaking contact. He walked to his desk, sat down heavily. 'Your self-will is too strong. There is no way back. Sainthood is behind you.'

'Then I'll die,' she said flatly, opening her eyes. 'Will you aid me?'

'I dislike this kind of thing. I don't usually—'

'Please.'

He sighed. 'All right.'

'Thank you, Reader Sterning.'

And he killed her.

3
Morgan

The laser sliced into the right front wheelhousing of Morgan's landcar and he lost control. Another beam sizzled along the door as he rolled free of the car. It slewed into a ditch, overturned, flamed, and exploded. The heavy smoke screened him as Morgan worked his way along the ditch, a fuse pistol in his right hand. Not much good against beam-guns, but his other weapons had been destroyed with the car.

The screening smoke worked both ways; he couldn't see *them*, verify their number. But maybe he could slip around them. It was quite possible they believed him dead in the explosion.

He was wrong about that.

A chopping blow numbed his left shoulder. Morgan hit ground, rolled, brought up the fuser, fired. His assailant fell back, grunting in pain. Morgan whipped up the pistol in a swift arc, catching a second enemy at chin-level, firing again. Which did the job.

Morgan rubbed circulation back into his numbed shoulder, his body pressed close in against the night-chilled gravel at the edge of the road. Behind him, in a flare of orange, the landcar continued to burn. He listened for further movement. Were there more of them out there, ready to attack him?

No sound. Nothing. No more of them. Only two, both dead now.

He took their beamers, checked the bodies. Both young, maybe fifteen to seventeen. Probably brothers, but Morgan couldn't tell for sure, since the face was mostly gone on the smaller one. At close range, a fuser is damned effective.

Morgan recharged the pistol and inspected the beam-guns, breaking them down. They were fine. He could use them.

It was too late to find another car. Better to sleep by the lake and go on in the morning.

The lake would be good. It would cool him out, ease some of the tension which knotted his muscles. He'd grown up near lakes like this one, fishing and swimming them with Jim Decker. Ole Jimbo. Poor unlucky bastard. The police got him in Detroit, lasered him down in a warehouse. Jimbo never believed he could die. Well, thought Morgan, we *all* die—sooner or later.

Lake Lotawana lay just ahead, less than a mile through the trees. Morgan threaded the woods, slid down the leaf-cloaked banking to the edge of the water. The lake flickered like soft flame, alive with moonlight. Morgan bent to wash his face and hands; the water rippled and stirred as he cupped it, cold and crystalline.

He drew the clean air of September into his lungs. Good autumn air, smelling of maple and oak. He savoured the smells of Missouri earth, of autumn grass and trees. A night bird cried out across the dark lake water.

Morgan hoped he would live long enough to reach Kansas City and do what he was sent to do. He could easily have been killed in the landcar explosion—or in Illinois, Ohio, Pennsylvania, or a few nights ago in Kansas. They'd been close on his tracks most of the way.

He prepared a bed of leaves, spreading dry twigs in a circle around it for several feet in each direction. The twigs would alert him to approaching enemies. Morgan lay down with a beamer at his elbow. Tomorrow, he would find another car and reach Kansas City. The girl and the money would be waiting there. He smiled and closed his eyes.

Morgan was sleeping deeply when they came down the bank, shadows among shadows, moving with professional stealth. They knelt beyond the circle of twigs and began scooping the branches away quietly. They planned to use blades, and that meant close body contact.

Morgan heard them at the last instant and rolled sideways, snatching up the beamer as he rolled. Too late. They were on him in a mass of unsheathed steel.

He broke free, stumbled, dropped the useless weapon, blood rushing to fill his open mouth. Morgan folded both hands across his stomach. 'I ...' He spoke to them as they watched him. 'I'm a dead man.'

And he fell backward as the dark waters of the lake, rippling, accepted his lifeless body.

4
David

'I *hate* bookstores,' said David.

'You're still a child,' his Guardian told him. 'As an adult, you'll see the value in books.'

David, who was eleven, allowed himself to be guided into the store. You don't get anywhere if you argue with a Guardian.

'May I be of service?' A tall old man smiled at them, dressed in the long grey robe of Learning.

'This is David,' said the Guardian, 'and he is here to rent a book.'

The old man nodded. 'And what is your choice, David?'

'I don't have one,' said David. 'Let Guardian decide.'

'Very well, then ...' The Bookman smiled again. 'Might I suggest some titles?'

'Please do,' said the Guardian.

The old man pursed his lips. 'Ah ... what about *Moby Dick?* Splendid seafaring adventure, laced with symbolic philosophy.'

'I hate whales,' said David. 'Sea things are disgusting.'

'Hmmm. Then I shall bypass Mr. Melville and Mr. Verne.

Let us move along to Dylan Thomas and his spirited *Under Milk Wood.*'

'Let's hear part of it,' said David.

The old man pressed a button on the wall and a door opened. A rumpled figure stepped into the room. His nose was red and bulbous; his hair was wild. He walked towards them, voice booming. He spoke of a small town by night, starless and bible-black, and of a wood 'limping invisible down to the sloeblack, slow, black, crow-black, fishingboat-bobbing sea.'

'I don't like it,' said David flatly. 'Send him back.'

'That will be all, Mr. Thomas,' said the Bookman.

The rumpled figure turned and vanished behind the door.

'I want a hunting story of olden times,' said David. 'Do you have any?'

'Naturally. We have many. What about *Big Woods?*'

'Who wrote that?' asked David.

'Mr. Faulkner. You'll like him, I'm sure.'

David shrugged, and the Bookman pressed another button. A tall man with sad eyes and a bristled moustache stepped into view. He spoke, with a drawl, of woods and rivers and loamed earth, and of 'the rich deep black alluvial soil which would grow cotton taller than the head of a man on a horse.'

'We'll take him,' said David.

'Indeed we will,' said the Guardian.

'Splendid,' said the Bookman.

William Faulkner waited quietly while the rental sheet was signed, then walked out with them.

'There is a story in my book,' he said to David, 'which I have titled "The Bear." Do you wish to hear it?'

'Sure. I want to hear the whole book if it's all about hunting.'

'The boy has a strange fascination with death,' the Guardian said to Mr. Faulkner.

'Then I shall begin with page one,' drawled the tall man as they were crossing a gridway.

David, looking up into the sad eyes of William Faulkner,

did not see the gridcar jetting towards him. The Guardian screamed and clawed at the boy's coat to pull him back, but was not successful. The car struck David, killing him instantly.

'Am I to be returned?' asked Mr. Faulkner.

5
Bax

They were having a shrimp curry at the Top of the Mark in San Francisco when the sharks began to bother the girl.

'They're so *close,*' she said. 'Why are they so close?'

Bax snapped his fingers. A waiter appeared at their table. 'Do something about those damn things,' Bax demanded.

'I'm very sorry, sir, but our repel shielding has temporarily failed.'

'Can you fix it?'

'Oh, of course, sir. That's being attended to now. We have the situation under control. At any moment the shielding should be fully operational.'

Bax waved him away. 'Are you satisfied?' he asked the girl.

She picked at her food, head lowered. 'I just won't look at them,' she said.

The sharks continued to bump the transparent outer shell, while a huge Manta Ray rippled through the jewelled waters. Far below, streaks of rainbow fish swarmed in and around the quake-tumbled ruins of office buildings, and the lichen-carpeted trucks and cable cars. An occasional divecab sliced past the restaurant, crowded with tourists.

Bax leaned across the table to take the girl's hand; his eyes softened. 'I thought you'd enjoy it here. This place is an exact duplicate of the original. You get a fantastic view of the city.'

'I feel trapped,' she admitted. 'I'm a surface girl, Bax. I don't like being here.'

Bax grinned. 'To tell you the truth, I don't like it much myself. But, at the moment, we really don't have any choice.'

'I know.' She gave his hand a squeeze. 'And it's all right. It's just that I—'

'Look,' Bax cut in. 'They've fixed it.'

The nuzzling sharks thrashed back abruptly as the energized shielding was reactivated. The outer dome now pulsed radiantly, silvering the sea. The sharks retreated deeper into the green-black Pacific.

'It's something about their teeth,' the girl said to Bax. 'Like thousands of upthrust knives . . .'

'Well, they're gone now. Forget them. Eat your curry.'

'When is the contact meeting us?' she asked.

'He's overdue. Should be here any minute.'

'You don't think anything's wrong, do you?'

Bax shook his head. 'What *could* be wrong?' He patted the inside of his coat. 'I have the stuff. They pay us for it and we leave San Fran for the islands. Take a long vacation. Enjoy what we've earned.'

'What about a crossup?' Her voice was intense. 'What if they hired another agent to take the stuff and dispose of you?'

He laughed. 'You mean dispose of *us*, don't you?'

The girl stared at him coldly. 'No. I mean you, Bax.'

Bax dropped his half-empty wine glass. 'You lousy bitch,' he said softly, slumping forward across the table.

The girl darted her hand into his coat, withdrew a small packet, and placed it inside her evening bag as a waiter rushed towards them.

'I think my husband has just had a heart seizure,' she said. 'I'll go for a doctor.'

And she calmly left the bar.

Outside, beyond the silvered fringe of light, the knife-toothed sharks circled the dome.

6
Lynda

The wind was demented; it whiplashed the falling snow into Lynda's eyes, into her half-open mouth as she stood, head raised to the storm, taking it in, allowing it to engulf her. The collar of her stormcoat was open and the cold snow needled her skin.

Then the wall glowed. Someone wanted her.

Annoyed, she killed the blizzard. The wind ceased. The snow melted instantly. The ceiling-sky was, once again, blue and serene above her head. She stepped from the Weather-chamber, peeling her stormcoat and boots.

Her father was there, looking his usual dour self.

'Sorry to break into your weather, Lynda, but I must talk to you.'

She walked to the barwall, pressed an oak panel, and an iced Scotch glided into her hand. 'Drink?' she offered.

'You know I never drink on the job.'

She sipped at the Scotch. 'I see. You're in town on a contract.'

'That's right.'

'I think it's revolting.' She shook her head. 'Why don't you get out of this business? You're too old to go on killing. You'll make a mistake and one of your contracts will end up doing *you* in. It happens all the time.'

'Not to me it won't,' said Lynda's father. 'I know my job.'

'It's sickening.'

The older man grunted. 'It's provided you with everything you've ever wanted.'

'And I guess I should be humbly grateful. As the pampered daughter of a high-level professional assassin, I'm very rich and very spoiled. I am, in fact, a totally worthless addition to society, thanks to you.'

'Then you shouldn't mind leaving it,' he said.

'What is *that* supposed to mean?'

'It means, dearest daughter, that my contract this trip is on you.'

And the beamgun he held beneath his coat took off Lynda's head.

The pattern is fixed. It's hopeless.

You don't want to try again?

To what purpose? Each time one of us penetrates, he's rejected. This planet does not want us. We'll have to move beyond the system.

Would the host bodies have survived without us?

Everyone on Earth dies eventually. But we trigger quick, violent death. It's their way of rejecting us. We must accept the pattern.

I liked the girl in New York ... Tris. And the little boy, David. We could have flowered in them.

The universe is immense. We'll find a host planet that's benign. Where we'll be welcome.

We're leaving Earth's orbit now.

The stars are waiting for us. A billion billion suns!

I love you!

THE ELLENA MOVEMENT

Nothing was happening.

It was no good, simply no damn good.

Hendy Joerdon grumpily untangled himself from the eroticizer's silken grasp and palmed the lustkill switch.

'Well, we all have our off nights,' sighed the inflatagirl as she brightly folded herself back into the unit. 'Even Gable did.'

Joerdon didn't know who the hell Gable was and said so.

'Gable, Clark. Public lust symbol. Twentieth century,' supplied the eroticizer. The girl was completely folded away by now and couldn't supply anything. 'How about a nice oily back rub instead?' The fat red machine eased closer to Joerdon's bed, visor plates gleaming. 'Release all those taut muscles. Loosey goosey!'

'Keep your damn rubberoids off me,' Joerdon told it. He suspected the machine of deviant behaviour and was in no mood to wrestle with it tonight. 'I need sleep.'

'You're out of shape, in my opinion,' the unit told him. 'Way out, I'd say.'

'Brass off,' said Joerdon.

The unit retired noiselessly as Hendy's bed rocked and soothed and babied him. 'Yum, yum, yum,' said the bed. 'Sleepums *good*.'

The next morning, at Deepfizz, Joerdon's desk told him he looked frettled.

'That's gollywop!' Joerdon snapped. He jogged a quick circle around the office. 'Just check those leg reflexes!'

'Boss wants you,' said a voice behind him. It was McWhirter, the officious ferret-faced pill brother in charge of moon popping.

'I'm having water,' Hendy growled, moving to the cooler.

'My, aren't we tense and testy,' grinned McWhirter. He peered closely at Joerdon. 'Have a sour night?'

Joerdon shrugged.

'It's the eyes,' said McWhirter. 'They always give you away. The eyes go puffy. Fatty tissue buildup. Sad . . . really sad.'

And he moused away.

'I hate that ferret-faced son-of-a-bitch,' Joerdon said to the water cooler.

'Open wide,' directed the boss.

Hendy opened his mouth, lolled his tongue, feeling puppy-like and vulnerable.

'Yes. Greyish, not pinkish.' The boss clucked. 'And it's got a wrinkle in the middle.'

'What does that mean?'

'Constriction. System's all bunched up and constricted.' The boss rolled to and fro across the desk. He was entirely egg-shaped and featureless, which made it hard to tell what his mood was. After an unhappy experience at Surestop, Joerdon had vowed never again to work for an egg-shaped boss. But progress had caught up with him. The old, affable cube-shaped boss who'd hired him at Deepfizz had been replaced, and there was nothing Joerdon could do about that.

Or about a lot of other things.

'You're frettled, Joerdon. Sit down and tell me what's frettling you.'

Joerdon sat down in a snugglechair. He sighed, shaking his head. 'Just a passing mood, sir.'

Executing a neat figure-eight pattern, the boss looped over to a saucer-shaped depression in his desk and egged into it. 'You're a popper five now, with a lot of responsibility. I don't need to tell you that Deepfizz wants its poppers unfrettled.'

'Yes, sir.' The snugglechair pressed Hendy's left buttock reassuringly.

'We didn't pull ahead of Dizzdrop point one forty-six to point one forty-five in national ratings last month by accident, Joerdon. Dizzdroppers are now becoming Deepfizzers at the rate of one every fiftieth centisecond—and we're *proud* of that statistic. Aren't you proud of that statistic, Joerdon?'

'I certainly am, sir,' said Hendy. The snugglechair squeezed his other buttock. It didn't help. Actually, Joerdon found it irritating.

The boss rolled leisurely back over the desk, stopped at the edge, tilted towards Joerdon. His tone became conspiratorial. 'Son ... have you popped? We'll find out soon enough, you know. Can't be hidden. If you *have* popped, just admit it.'

'Oh, no, sir! I'd never—'

'Good! Delighted to hear it,' said the boss. 'One cannot continue to help guide society when one loses one's *self*-guidance. A popping popper is a public disgrace!'

'Yo, yo!' Hendy said with alacrity, using the official form of affirmation.

'Maybe you ought to have a medcheck, just to be sure everything's acey,' suggested the boss.

Hendy agreed.

'Visit Doc Sidge at the end of your work sesh. Get a run-through. Then come see me in the morn. We'll fab more then.' The egg-shaped boss rolled over to his basket slot and dropped abruptly out of sight.

Working with his pill brothers in the huge pink Deepfizz adlab, Joerdon told himself that he was basically acey—that he had a right to a bout of moodiness after losing Ellena. They had been set for a procreation sesh when she suddenly vanished. Here one day, working next to him radiant and fresh—gone the next. When Joerdon asked what had become of her, the ferret-faced McWhirter had smirked. 'Maybe she popped!'

'Not on your bizzle!' Hendy had snapped back. 'Not Ellena!'

But he'd given it a lot of thought. *Had* she popped? That would explain her disappearance. Popped poppers were banished, sent outside. A nasty end to public service.

Joerdon knew he hadn't been pulling his weight at Deepfizz over the past week since Ellena vanished. Most of his Marspop copy had ended in deadwaste. Flushed with sudden guilt, Joerdon stared morosely at the huge wallglow tri-mural of Hately Hately. Spade-bearded and rock-nosed, Hately of Deepfizz—the true giant of the twenty-first century. And beneath, carved in letters of bronze, his fabled words: 'A STONED NATION IS A HAPPY NATION.' The big habit had solved all problems. War was eliminated and sex, as removed from lust—which was properly supplied by the eroticizer—was now a strict religious rite, reserved, at specified intervals, for vital procreation among Deepfizz-Dizzdrop personnel. Which was, Joerdon knew, as it should be.

He attempted to concentrate on his work, but found himself thinking dismally of Ellena for the remainder of his data-pop period.

'Ouch,' said Joerdon as he was thumped and pumped, tapped and grasped and twisted and analysed by the med-check run-through unit. 'Ouch,' he said several more times.

'Nothing,' said the unit, hopping back in a bird-like motion. 'Nothing, nothing, nothing, nothing. You have nothing wrong with you.'

'You sound disappointed.'

'And why not? My job is to find things wrong with people, so I can send them to Doc Sidge.'

'Where is he? I think I should talk to him.'

'Sidge sees only sickos,' the unit told him. 'You are *not* a sicko. All you have is a temporary psychological imbalance caused by mild emotional multistress. And that, sadly enough from my viewpoint, will pass. Good tubing.'

'Good tubing,' Joerdon said to the unit.

He left carrying a medstamped diskslip which certified that he was in ideal physical condition.

Naturally, there was no trace of Deepfizz in his blood.

The boss would be pleased.

'Psssst!'

'What did you say?'

'I said "Psssst!"'

'Nobody ever says "Psssst!' anymore,' Joerdon explained to the crouching tube rider next to him.

'I'm attempting to be secretive. I'm sure some people still say "Psssst!" when they are attempting to be secretive.'

'I won't argue the point,' said Joerdon.

The tube rider was small and dark and furry. He smelled odd. 'I've been outside,' he whispered.

Joerdon stared at him. He'd never seen an outsider inside. 'But that's not legal. None of us go outside unless we pop. Then we're *sent* outside. There are no outside insiders, nor inside outsiders.'

The furry little tube rider snorted. 'That's just the poddlecock they feed you industry people. I know things you *don't*.'

Joerdon glanced nervously around the humming tuber.

No other riders this early. And luckily, on this model, the seats couldn't talk. 'Why tell me this?'

'A lady wants you.'

'What lady?'

'Lady Ellena Nubbins, who else?'

Joerdon gripped the man's furry front. 'What do you know of Miss Nubbins? Where is she?'

'Outside,' the unflustered tuber replied, 'and she wants you with her.'

Joerdon shuddered. He knew what it was like out there. Unstable. Odd-smelling. Full of goofy pill-poppers. He'd seen them on the scope, mooning in the streets, popping their hours away. And now Ellena—sober, dedicated, hardworking Ellena Nubbins—was one of them. His worst suspicions had been verified. It was obviously no use going out to her. Once a popped popper, always a popped popper. Addiction was immediate.

'Tell her that I still regard her with considerable affection, that her leaving has severely upset my work, but that I shall *never* join her.'

'Is that final?'

'Indeed it is,' nodded Joerdon.

'Then, let's try a blitz on the bizzle.'

Joerdon was astonished when the furry man tried exactly that.

Joerdon woke up inside a zebra-striped anachronism.

'Wok!' he said, clearing his throat. His head swam, settled; he blinked rapidly. 'Wok!' he said again, unsteadily.

'You'll be acey soon,' said a furry voice. The little tube man was cradling Joerdon's head in his odd-smelling lap. Hendy pushed himself into a sitting position.

He looked out a window. They were moving over the streets of New York. That's when he found out he was riding inside an anachronism: a 1971 Cadillac, zebra-striped.

'Our movement supervisor is responsible,' said the ex-tube rider. 'He restored this old Caddie, right down to her last lug nut. Even the exhaust fumes are properly poisonous. It's the work of a craftsman.'

'I didn't know they allowed automobiles in New York,' said Joerdon. 'Aren't these things against the law?' He squinted at the driver in the forward seat, but the man was hatted and swaddled and Hendy couldn't make out any physical details.

'Puddlecod!' said his furry friend. 'With the lawboys stoned, nobody's left to tell anybody anything. Cities are falling apart. Last week, the Empire State Building fell down flat and nobody said foof about it.'

'I didn't scan that on the scope.'

'There are lots you don't scan on the scope. You insiders are bizzle-cleshed. You see only what the industry wants you to see.'

Joerdon asked, 'Where are we going?'

'To clan HQ,' said the furry one. 'Just sit back and enjoy the ride.'

A classic .45-calibre slug smashed through the Cadillac's rear window, barely missing Joerdon's bizzle.

'Ooops!' said the muffled driver. He stopped the car, quickly leaped out, and sprayed a noisily advancing crowd with concentrated laser-beam fire. Then he hopped back in and resumed driving.

'Who were *they*?' Joerdon wanted to know.

'Zealots. Bishops, cardinals, ex-nuns, and the like. Bothersome. They fire classic slugs from restored museum pistols at you. We have to show them who's boss. They can get pesky. Nothing unusual though. All part of the general civic breakdown.'

The car swerved to avoid a sleeping Deepfizzer in the centre of Fifth Avenue. Others, along the walks, chanted at the Cad, 'Toe to tip, tip to toe, pip-pop as you go!'

The furry man ignored them. 'We headquarter at Tiffany's,' he said. 'Lends a little class to the operation.'

They parked directly in front of the famous jewellery store. The driver heh-heh'd under his swaddle. 'I always get a kick out of parking in the red zone.' He led them inside.

Joerdon still couldn't make out the man's face, but the tips of his ears looked vaguely familiar.

'Where's Ellena?'

'Here, Hendy!'

She ran towards him across a marbled floor, arms extended, aglitter in diamonds and emeralds and pearls and sapphires.

They rubbed groins happily, and Joerdon felt the old procreation urge welling up. Suddenly he pushed her back.

'You want me to pop but I won't. Not even for you. I won't. Won't. Won't. Won't. Will not.'

She giggled, dislodging a diamond tiara from her hair. It clattered unnoticed to the veined marble.

'Meet the chief.' The furry man and the still-swaddled driver gripped Hendy's elbows and quickmarched him into a large, deep-carpeted office at the rear of the building. A panelled side door slid open and the chief stepped into view.

Joerdon gasped. 'McWhirter!'

'No other,' said McWhirter.

'You're an outsider!'

McWhirter smirked. 'Have been for the past couple of years.'

'What ... where ... why ... how?'

'Good questions. But first'—he gestured expansively—'let me introduce the principal members of the movement. My furry, odd-smelling assistant is Fedor Bandlecliff Bumpums, a biochemist of marked brilliance. And doubtless you already know the swaddled gentleman who drove you here.'

The swaddled driver unswaddled.

Joerdon gasped. 'Doc Sidge!'

'No other,' said Sidge.

'I *thought* I recognized your distinctive ear tips.'

McWhirter put one arm around Ellena. 'And Miss Nubbins is a pivotal member. She joined our movement quite recently, as you know.'

'And you've kidnapped me to become part of your illegal, subversive, clandestine group, is that it?'

'More or less,' replied McWhirter. 'Eventually we would

have kidnapped you anyway, but we kidnapped you *now* because dear Ellena wanted you outside, with her. I thought Fedor B. Bumpums told you that inside the tuber.'

'I simply won't pop. Not for all the drickle in New York. Do with me what you will, but I shall not betray my heritage.'

'But,' said Ellena, 'nobody wants you to. None of us pop. we're *anti*poppers.'

'I don't—'

'You don't understand,' said Doc Sidge.

McWhirter sighed. 'Tell him, Ellena, while I go put on some rubies. I love wearing rubies in the afternoon.' He loped away over the thick carpet.

Ellena smiled patiently. 'We are building a drug-free movement to overthrow the Deepfizz-Dizzdrop industry.'

'Great hobble!'

'Naturally, you're surprised.' She removed her outer garments as she talked. Then her inner garments. Then her inner-inner outer garments and, finally, her outer-inners.

Ellena was stark naked and looked particularly appealing.

'You're ... particularly appealing, you know,' Joerdon could not help saying.

'That's the whole smidge,' she said, swaying towards him. Doc and the furry biochemist slyly skittered from the room.

'Is—is this an unofficial procreation sesh?' asked Hendy.

'Not exactly, but it may end up that way. The purpose is just to jizz.'

'I begin to see your point,' said Hendy, shucking his outer garments.

'What we do is stay straight and help other people kick the big habit,' she husked in a smoky tone. 'Also, we kidnap bizzle-cleshed industry insiders and turn them into straight, *un*bizzle-cleshed outsiders. Pretty soon, when enough insiders become outsiders—all jizzing each other for the good of mankind—then people slowly rediscover the joys of the movement and the industry breaks down and we have a truly free society. Isn't that wonderfully simple?'

'It's simply wonderful,' declared Hendy, squeezing a

deftly weighted breast. 'It's also a hell of a lot of fun.'

And, without further urging, Hendy Joerdon enthusiastically joined the movement.

BUT I HAVE PROMISES TO KEEP ...

Alone within the humming ship, deep in its honey-combed metal chambers, Murdock waited for death. While the rocket moved inexorably towards Earth—an immense silver needle threading the dark fabric of space—he waited calmly through the final hours, knowing that the verdict was absolute, that hope no longer existed.

Electronically self-sufficient, the ship was doing its job perfectly, the job it had been built to do. After twenty years in space, the ship was taking Robert Murdock home.

Home. Earth. Thayerville, a small town in Kansas. Clean air, a shaded street, and a white, two-storey house near the end of the block. Home after two decades among the stars.

The rocket knifed through the black of space, its atomics, like a great heartbeat, pulsing far below Robert Murdock as he sat quietly before a round port, seeing and not seeing the endless darkness surrounding him.

Murdock was remembering.

He remembered the worried face of his mother, her whispered prayers for his safety, the way she held him close for a long, long moment before he mounted the ship's ramp those twenty years ago. He remembered his father: a tall, weathered man, and that last crushing handshake before he said goodbye.

It was almost impossible to realize that they were now old and white-haired, that his father was forced to use a cane, that his mother was bowed and wasted by the years.

And what of himself?

He was now forty-one—and space had weathered him as the plains of Kansas had weathered his father. He, too, had fought storms in his job beyond Earth, terrible, alien storms; worse than any he had ever encountered on his own planet. And he, too, had laboured on plains under burning suns far stronger than Sol. His face was square and hard-featured, his eyes dark and buried beneath thrusting ledges of bone.

Robert Murdock removed the stero-shots of his parents from his uniform pocket and studied their faces. Warm, smiling, *waiting* faces: waiting for their son to come home to them. Carefully, he unfolded his mother's last letter. She had always been stubborn about sending tapes, complaining that her voice was unsteady, that she found it so difficult to speak her thoughts into the metallic mouth of a cold, impersonal machine. She insisted on using an old-fashioned pen, forming the words slowly in an almost archaic script. He had received this last letter just before his take-off for Earth, and it read:

Dearest,

We are so excited! You father and I listened to your voice again and again, telling us that you are coming home to us at last, and we both thanked our good Lord that you were safe. Oh, we are so eager to see you, son. As you know, we have not been too well of late. Your father's heart doesn't allow him to get out much any more. Even the news that you are coming back to us has over-excited him. Then, of course, my own health seems none too good as I suffered another fainting spell last week. But there is no real cause for alarm—and you are not to worry!—since Dr. Thom says I am quite strong, and that these spells will pass. I am, however, resting as much as possible, so that I will be fine when you arrive. Please, Bob, come back to us safely. We pray God you will come home safe and well. The thought of you fills our hearts each day. Our lives are suddenly rich again. Hurry, Bob. Hurry!

All our love,
Mother

Robert Murdock put the letter aside and clenched his fists. Only brief hours remained to him—and Earth was *days* away. The town of Thayerville was an impossible distance across space; he knew he could never reach it alive.

Once again, as they had so many times in the recent past, the closing lines of the ancient poem by Robert Frost came whispering through his mind:

But I have promises to keep,
And miles to go before I sleep . . .

He'd promised that he would come home, and he would keep that promise. Despite death itself, he would return to Earth.

The doctors had shown him that it was impossible. They had charted his death; they had told him when his heart would stop beating, when his breathing would cease. Death, for Robert Murdock, was a certainty. His alien disease was incurable.

But they had listened to his plan. They had listened, and agreed.

Now, with less than a half-hour of life remaining, Murdock was walking down one of the ship's long corridors, his bootheels ringing on the narrow metal walkway.

He was ready, at last, to keep his promise.

Murdock paused before a wall storage locker, twisted a small dial. A door slid smoothly back. He looked up at the tall man standing motionless in the darkness. Reaching forward, Murdock make a quick adjustment.

The tall man stepped smoothly down into the corridor; the light flashed in the deep-set eyes, almost hidden under thrusting ledges of bone. The man's face was hard and square-featured. 'You see,' he smiled, 'I *am* perfect.'

'And so you are,' said Murdock. But then, he reflected, everything *depends* on perfection. There must be no flaw, however small. None.

'My name is Robert Murdock,' said the tall figure in the neat spaceman's uniform. 'I am forty-one years of age, sound of mind and body. I have been in space for two decades—and now I am going home.'

Murdock smiled, a tight smile of triumph which flickered briefly across his tired face.

'How much longer?' the tall figure asked.

'Ten minutes. Perhaps a few seconds beyond that,' said Murdock slowly. 'They told me it would be painless.'

'Then ...' The tall man paused, drew in a long breath. 'I'm sorry.'

Murdock smiled again. He knew that a machine, however perfect, could not experience the emotion of sorrow—but it eased him to hear the words.

He'll be fine, thought Murdock. He'll serve in my place and my parents will never suspect that I have not come home to them. A month, as arranged, and the machine would turn itself in to company officials on Earth. Yes, Murdock thought, he will be fine.

'Remember,' said Murdock, 'when you leave them, they *must* believe you are going back into space.'

'Naturally,' said the machine. 'When the month I am to stay with them has passed, they'll see me board a rocket. They'll see it fire away from Earth, outbound, and they'll know that I cannot return for two more decades. They will accept the fact that their son must return to space—that a healthy spaceman cannot leave the Service until he has reached sixty. Let me assure you, all will go exactly as you have planned.'

It *will* work, Murdock told himself; every detail has been taken into consideration. The android possesses every memory that I possess; his voice is *my* voice, his small habits my own. And when he leaves them, when it appears that he has gone back to the stars, the pre-recorded tapes of mine will continue to reach them from space, exactly as they have in the past. Until their deaths. They will never know I'm gone.

'Are you ready now?' the tall figure asked softly.

'Yes,' said Murdock, nodding. 'I'm ready.'

And they began to walk slowly down the long corridor.

Robert Murdock remembered how proud his parents had been when he was accepted for Special Service. He had been the only boy in the entire town of Thayerville to be chosen. It had been a great day! The local band playing, the mayor —old Mr. Harkness with those little glasses tilted across his nose—making a speech, telling everyone how proud Thayerville was of its chosen son . . . and his mother crying because she was so happy.

But then, it was only right that he should have gone into space. The other boys, the ones who failed to make the grade, had not *lived* the dream as he had lived it. From the moment he had watched the first rocket land, he had known, beyond any possible doubt, that he would become a spaceman. He had stood there in that cold December of 1980, a boy of twelve, watching the rocket fire down from space, watching it thaw and blacken the frozen earth. And he had known, in his heart, that he would one day follow it back to the stars. From that moment on, he had dreamed only of moving up and away from Earth, away to vast and alien horizons, to wondrous worlds beyond imagining.

And many of the others had been unwilling to give up *everything* for space. Even now, after two decades, he could still hear Julie's words: *'Oh, I'm sure you love me, Bob, but not enough. Not nearly enough to give up your dream.'* And she had left him, gone out of his life because she knew there was no room in it for her. There was only space—deep space and the rockets and the burning stars. Nothing else.

He remembered his last night on Earth, twenty years ago, when he had felt the pressing immensity of the vast universe surrounding him as he lay in his bed. He remembered the sleepless hours before dawn—when he could feel the tension building within the small white house, within himself lying there in the heated stillness of the room. He remembered the rain, near morning, drumming the roof and the thunder roaring across the Kansas sky. And then, somehow, the thunder's roar blended into the atomic roar of a rocket, carrying him away from Earth, away to the far stars . . . away . . .

Away.

*

The tall figure in the neat spaceman's uniform closed the outer airlock and watched the body drift into blackness. The ship and the android were one; a pair of complex and perfect machines doing their job.

For Robert Murdock the journey was over, the long miles had come to an end.

Now he would sleep forever in space.

When the rocket landed, on a bright Kansas morning in July, the crowds were there, waving and shouting out Murdock's name. The city officials were all present to the last man, each with a carefully rehearsed speech; the town band sent brassy music into the blue sky and children waved flags. Then a hush fell over the assembled throng. The atomic engines had stilled and the airlock was sliding back.

Robert Murdock appeared, tall and heroic in a splendid dress uniform which threw back the light of the sun in a thousand glittering patterns. He smiled and waved as the crowd burst into fresh shouting and applause.

And, at the far end of the ramp, two figures waited: an old man, bowed and trembling over a cane, and a seamed and wrinkled woman, her hair blowing white, her eyes shining.

When the tall man finally reached them, pushing his way through pressing lines of well-wishers, they embraced him feverishly, clinging tight to his arms.

Their son had returned. Robert Murdock had come home from space.

'Well,' said a man at the fringe of the crowd, 'there they go.'

His companion sighed and shook his head. 'I *still* don't think it's right somehow. It just doesn't seem right to me.'

'It's what they wanted, isn't it?' asked the other. 'It's what they wrote in their wills. They vowed their son would never come home to death. In a month he'll be gone anyway. Back for another twenty years. Why ruin it all for him?' The man paused, shading his eyes against the sun. 'And they *are* perfect, aren't they? He'll never know.'

'I suppose you're right,' nodded the second man. 'He'll never know.'

And he watched the old man and the old woman and the tall son until they were out of sight.

COINCIDENCE

When Harry Dobson's wife suggested they spend their last night together (before Harry's trip) in a New York hotel he agreed. It was to be a kind of instant second honeymoon, and Harry savoured the drive down from Westport with his wife cuddled close to him. It reminded Harry of the early days, before the house and kids had aged them both. The kids were grown and gone, but the house in Westport, with its high upkeep and higher taxes, dragged at Harry like a weight. He enjoyed the overnight stay in a New York hotel, enjoyed the sexual passion he was still able to inspire in Margaret.

What Harry Dobson *didn't* enjoy was having his wife bump him awake with a naked hip at 6 a.m. in the morning.

'What's wrong?' he wanted to know.

'It's the man in the next room,' whispered Margaret, pressing close to him in the double bed. 'He's been moaning. He woke me up.'

'So he's probably sick, maybe drunk. Who cares?'

'It's what he's moaning that spooks me,' said Margaret. 'I want you to hear him. I think he's some kind of maniac.'

'Okay, okay,' Harry grunted. And he listened to the agonized words which filtered through the thin walls of the hotel room.

'I've killed,' moaned the man. 'I've killed. I've killed.'

'He keeps repeating that over and over,' Margaret whispered. 'I think you'd better do something.'

'Do what?' asked Harry, propping himself against the

pillow to light a cigarette. 'Maybe he's just having a bad dream.'

'But he keeps saying it over and over. It really spooks me. We could be next door to a murderer.'

'So what do you suggest?'

She blinked at him, absently stroking her left breast. 'Call the manager. Have someone investigate.'

Harry sighed, kicked off the blankets and padded barefoot to the house phone on the dresser. He picked up the receiver, waited for the switchboard to acknowledge.

'This is Harry Dobson in room 203. There's a character next door who's moaning about having killed somebody. He's been keeping us awake. Yeah ... he's in 202. Right next door.'

Harry listened, holding the phone, slowly stubbing out his cigarette on the glass top of the dresser.

'What's happening?' asked Harry's wife.

'They're checking to see who's in 202.'

'He's stopped moaning,' she said.

'No, no,' said Harry into the receiver. '*I'm* in 203. Okay, forget it, just forget it.'

He slammed down the phone.

'What's wrong?'

'The stupid idiot on the desk has my name down for *both* rooms!'

'Couldn't it be a coincidence?' Margaret asked. 'I mean, your name isn't *that* unusual. There must be several Harry Dobsons in New York.'

'Not door-to-door in the same damn hotel,' he said. 'Anyhow, they claim they can't do anything about the guy and unless he gets violent in there to just ignore him.' He shook his head. 'That's New York for you.'

'I think we'd better leave,' said Margaret. She got up and walked to the bathroom.

Harry blew out his breath in disgust, got his pants off the chair and began dressing. He was scheduled to fly back to L.A. this morning anyhow, so he'd get to the airport a little early. He could have breakfast there.

He and his wife left the hotel room.

In the elevator she told him she'd write him at least once a week while he was gone. He was sweet, she told him, and if it hadn't been for the maniac in 202 their night together would have been beautiful.

'Sure,' said Harry Dobson.

They said goodbye in the lobby. Then Harry checked out, giving the desk clerk hell for mixing up the room numbers.

'I represent a major firm,' he told the clerk. 'I'm an important man, damnit! What if someone wanted to reach me? My messages might have gone to a nut in 202. Do you understand me?'

The desk clerk said he was very sorry.

Harry walked out to a cab. Grey rain drizzled down from a soot-coloured sky and a chill November wind blew the rain against Harry's face.

'Kennedy airport,' he said to the driver. But before he climbed into the taxi he paused. *He's watching you. That bastard in 202 is watching you.* Harry shaded his eyes against the rain and peered upward at the second-floor street window of room 202.

A tall man was at the open window, ignoring the blowing rain, glaring down at him. The man's face was dark with anger.

Harry stared, unblinking. *Good grief, he even looks like me. Like an older version of me. No wonder the clerk mixed us up. Well, to hell with him!*

By the time his jet soared away from New York Harry Dobson put the man from 202 firmly out of his thoughts. Harry was concerned with the report he'd be making to the sales manager back in California. He was working out some statistics on a board in his lap when he happened to notice the passenger in the window seat directly across the aisle.

What—it's him! Can't be. Left him back in New York.

The passenger had been reading a magazine; now he raised his head and swung his eyes slowly towards Harry Dobson. Cold hatred flowed from those eyes.

The tourist section was only half filled and Harry had no

trouble getting another seat several rows back. Damned if he'd sit there and let this creep give him the evil eye. Maybe Margaret was right; maybe the guy *was* some kind of maniac.

At Los Angeles International Harry was the first passenger to disembark. Inside the airport building he arranged for a porter to collect his flight baggage. Then he waited for it in a cab near the door. Harry didn't want to risk running into the weirdo at the baggage pickup.

So far so good. The guy was nowhere in sight.

His baggage arrived and Harry tipped the porter and gave the taxi driver an address in West Los Angeles. As the car rolled on to the freeway Harry relaxed. Apparently the man had made no attempt to follow him. It was over.

Harry paid the driver, carried his bags into the rented apartment, took some Scotch from his briefcase and poured himself a drink. He felt fine now. He checked the window just to be certain the guy hadn't followed him. The street below was empty.

Harry unpacked, took his suits to the closet, opened the sliding door—and fell back, gasping.

The man was there, inside the closet. He stood in the darkness, smiling like a fiend. Then he dived at Harry's throat, hands closing on his windpipe. Harry kicked free, tumbled over a chair, twisting away from his attacker.

That's when the man pulled the knife from his belt.

Harry scrambled around the bed, putting space between himself and his attacker. No good trying for the door; the man would have him if he tried that.

'Who—are you?' gasped Harry. 'What—what do you want from me?'

'I want to kill you,' said the man, smiling. 'That's all you need to know.'

Keeping himself between Harry and the door he began slashing with the knife—ripping the blade into mattress, chairs, curtains, clothing—as Harry watched in numb terror.

But when the man pulled Margaret's photo from Harry's

briefcase, and drove the knife through it a red rage replaced the fear in Harry Dobson; the bastard was human, after all. Harry was ten years younger, stronger.

The man was half turned towards the bed when Harry struck him with a heavy table lamp. The other fell backward, stunned, dropping the knife.

'You crazy sonuvabitch,' Harry shouted, snapping up the knife and driving it into the man's back. Once. Twice. Three times. The man grunted, then did not move. Harry stood over him for a long, long moment—but he did not move again.

Who is he? Who the hell is he? Harry could find no identification on the body. He thought of calling the police but decided that was too risky. There were no witnesses. The apartment had not been burglarized nor were there signs of a forced entry. *Bastard must have had a key.* To the police it would appear that Harry Dobson had coldly murdered this man.

Insane! I don't even know him. Which is exactly why you must get rid of the body. Once he's gone there'll be no way to link you to his death.

That night Harry cleaned up the apartment, placed the blanket-wrapped corpse in the trunk of his car and drove out along the ocean, past Malibu, to a deserted stretch of beach—where he dumped the weighted body into the water.

He was a madman. Simply because you complained about him at the hotel he followed you to the West Coast and tried to kill you. You have no reason to feel guilt. Forget all this. Live your life and forget him.

Harry Dobson tried to do that. When his wife called him he didn't mention what had happened. And when his business trip ended he returned to New York, and resumed his life.

A decade passed. Each time the face of the dead man from 202 looked in his mind Harry Dobson shut down the vision. Finally he could look back upon the entire incident as a kind of bizarre dream. He felt neither guilt or fear.

Then, almost ten years to the month, Harry found himself

at the same hotel in New York. He was in town on his annual business trip and, this particular visit, had decided to stay at this hotel to prove that the ghost of the man he'd killed was truly exorcised.

In fact, to close the circle, he asked the clerk for the old room, 203.

'Sorry, sir, but that room is occupied. However, I can give you the one right next door to it, room 202. Will that be satisfactory?'

Irony. The dead man's room. All right, Harry said, that would be satisfactory.

Room 202 contained a double bed, white glass-topped dresser, circular table and chair, a standing brass lamp in the corner ... He remembered the furniture! But that was because it was the same, exactly the same, as 203. The rooms on this floor were no doubt identically furnished. The odd thing was that the decor hadn't been changed in ten years.

Harry took a fresh bottle of Scotch from his suitcase and poured a solid drink for himself. The Scotch eased him, reduced his tension. It was late, near midnight, and after several more belts of Scotch he was ready for sleep, amused at the drama of the situation, no longer tense at the prospect of sleeping in a room once occupied by a man he had stabbed to death.

Near morning, Harry began to mumble in his sleep. He was having a bad dream, a nightmare about being tired and convicted of murder. The attorney was hammering at him on the witness stand and Harry had broken under the verbal assault. 'I've killed,' he admitted. 'I've killed. I've killed.' Over and over. 'Killed ... killed ... killed ...'

He finally awoke, sweating, wide-eyed. *Wow, what a hellish dream! It's this room. That's what triggered it, allowed it to take control of my subconscious. But I'm all right now. I'm fine. The dream's over.*

He became aware of voices in 203 filtering through the thin wall of the room. A woman's voice, whispery but sharp, and upset. 'I think you'd better do something.'

'Do what?' asked a man's voice, muffled but distinct. 'Maybe he's just having a bad dream.'

'But he keeps saying it over and over. It really spooks me. We could be next door to a murderer.'

'So what do you suggest?'

'Call the manager. Have someone investigate.'

Harry heard the springs squeak as the man climbed out of bed. He heard him pick up the phone and say, 'This is Harry Dobson in room 203. There's a character next door who's moaning about having killed somebody . . .'

Harry didn't want to hear any more. He walked into the bathroom and vomited into the bowl, remaining on his knees until he heard the door finally slam in 203.

Then, shaking, he walked back into his room and called the desk. 'Who—who's registered in 203?'

'Uh . . . that's Mr. Dobson, sir. But he's checking out.'

'All right,' said Harry evenly. And he put down the phone.

He walked over to the street window, threw it open. Grey rain, whipped by a chill wind, blew in upon him, stinging his face.

A man came out of the hotel, hailed a cab. Just before he got into the taxi he turned to look up at Harry, shading his eyes against the wet. Younger. A face like his, but ten years younger. *The murdering bastard!* Harry glared down at him.

And when the man was gone, and he had called the airport to confirm his flight back to Los Angeles, Harry Dobson took the knife out of his suitcase and held it in his hand for a long, long moment.

Knowing, beyond any doubt, that he would eventually die by it.

FASTERFASTER!

When JamesTen teleported into the office wearing his twintone perforated Venusian breathingboots and a rakishly cut sports jacket in worsted plastic, Miss Manypiggies sobbed brokenly and threw herself into his arms. 'Rip off my clothing, James,' she pleaded. 'Love me, rape me, torture me, I don't care! Take my subtly tanned supple woman's body and—'

JamesTen pushed her gently aside. 'Not now, Manypiggies,' he husked in a silken voice reserved for love-crazed secretaries. 'Z wants me inside, where things count. God knows what's up in there, but it's my type of trouble. Now, be a sweet and buzz me in, chop-chop.'

'Chop-chop,' sighed Miss Manypiggies as JamesTen stepped lightly into the Matter Disintegrator. She thumbed the proper button and the suave secret agent wavered and vanished.

He reappered, all atoms neatly in place, beside Z's desk.

'Good to see you, Ten,' rumbled Z. His outwardly pleasant tone meant another joust with death was in the offing. JamesTen smiled thinly.

'Sorry for the delay in getting here, sir, but I was feeding mutated Shakespeare into my home computer.'

'More of your attempts to bring the Bard to the robot masses, eh, James?'

'That's the idea, sir. If we could educate these clumsy devils, feed *Robo and Juliet* into their receptors, the world would be a calmer place, sir. Peace has its roots in culture.'

'Idealistic claptrap and bushwah, Ten!'

JamesTen stiffened. The casual banter had ended.

Slowly, Z rocked back in his sleepchair, tenting his fingers. JamesTen tensed. When Z tented his fingers . . .

'Know anything about a man who calls himself Plugo Mittelholzer?'

''Fraid not, sir.'

'It's an assumed name—and he's used several others. Thiam Ghong. Elwood Beeles. Francis Fahrenkrug. Clifford Siggfoos. Raymond Tarbutton. Nickolaus Kronschnable. Orlando Pipes. Thomas Nuckles. Willie Ploughboy. Roman Belch. Cungee Arena. Vertie Cheatam. Elsworth Molder. Exie Moneylon. Chester Foat. Socorro Quankenbush. Pershing Threewit. Lester Hoots. George Fiebelkorn. Laurence Torrance. Kenneth Dankwardt. And, most recently, Simon

Brain.'

'Is Brain his real name, sir?'

'His real name, according to the Chekfax Team, is Sir Henry FasterFaster.'

'Odd name, that.'

'Exactly. And he is, beyond any doubt whatever, the most insanely dangerous man in the universe as we know it today. Of course, God knows what's *really* out there!'

'The Astrom boys are doing a first-rate job for us, sir. Discovered a brand new galaxy just last week. I took it upon myself to send a few junior agents out to clean it up. Alien scum and all that sort of thing, sir. Cut 'em to ribbons!'

'We're drifting, Ten.'

'Quite, sir.' Again the thin smile.

'Know anything about Operation Mibs?'

'Has it—by any remote chance, sir—something to do with *marbles?*'

'Exactly. Good show, Ten!' Z rocked back for a quick relaxing instant of sleep, then snapped his eyes open. 'Sir Henry Fasterfaster is engaged in what can only be termed a cosmic game of mibs.'

''Fraid you've lost me, sir.'

Z smiled his lizard's smile and lit a pseudocamel. 'I'll fill you in.'

JamesTen slipped into an attentionseat. It kept him bolt upright. One hundred and thirty-six straight hours at the computer had taken the edge off his thinking and this was no time to funk out.

'Sir Henry Fasterfaster is from Uranus,' began Z, his voice deceptively casual. 'The chap's mother was a sod-common, slug-stupid skin sorter in a Plutonian onion mine—and his father a trifinned out-of-work Slimecrawler from Neptune. I believe you call 'em Neppies.'

'Right, sir. Nasty devils. Low co-op potential.'

'At any rate these two ran away together and they mated —God knows *how*—producing Sir Henry. He was adopted by a team of Wogglebugs, schooled in a Jupe-based low-grade Unit, travelled the sawdust trail as part of an undersea juggling act, and peddled Lowdope in the Asteroids. Ended up here in Greater Olde England and proved himself a brilliant lad, taking his doctorate in Worm Pathology.'

'Sounds ordinary enough, sir.'

'Shut up and listen, you damned machine!'

JamesTen flushed. He did not like to be reminded that he was of android origin.

'At any rate, Fasterfaster was using worms for cover, nothing more. His game was a queer one.'

'Go on, sir.'

'You must understand, James, that Sir Henry was crazed from the outset, twisted with powerlust, consumed with an acid hatred for every living creature known to us at present, writhing with dark desires, bent on the most depraved form of ultimate revenge on the universe as we know it for the cruel joke his mismated parents had played upon him. He was, in short, *not* a normal student.'

'Sounds like Psyc fodder, sir.'

'Exactly. A brute and a fiend right enough. And ugly as sin. Great long leathery neck, toad's eyes, distended red-rimmed nostrils, purple hands, immense kangaroo feet, and no teeth at all. This was the legacy of his unnatural birth.'

'Think I'm beginning to get the picture, sir.'

'He's a past master at disguise. Can look bloody normal if he's about it. He's picked up a lot of awful tricks whilst kicking about the system. Lived on a dozen worlds before he was a post-teener. Hobnobbed with outcast mice on Jupiter. Stirred up the milk robots on Venus. Got a schoolmarm in trouble in Redding, Pennsylvania. She gave birth to a thing no doctor could look upon. They had to bury it, chop-chop. Nasty business all round.'

'What are you leading up to, sir?'

JamesTen was getting logy, despite the sharp prods from the attentionseat.

Z stubbed out his pseudocamel and leaned forward, fingers tented. 'JamesEight and JamesNine were destroyed by our ruthless friend. And they were the latest models. I've ordered two more just like them, but it takes an ungodly amount of time to assemble those damned killer machines. Oh—sorry, Ten.'

'No offence taken, sir.' JamesTen smiled thinly. No use in being fussy about discussing his talent; he was built to kill and he enjoyed killing. It was as simple as that. A prime ooooooooooooooo android could kill anything that moved anywhere, no questions asked. The extra o did it. A plain oooooooooooooo android was only licensed to cripple for life.

'What I'm leading up to, Ten, is this: the man who now calls himself Plugo Mittelholzer is right here in Greater New London, on the Strand. He's working a cover operation called E.T.T.T.P.U.—Economy Time Travel To Parallel Universes. A clever front for his master plan.'

'And that plan *is*, sir?' JamesTen's eyes were lidding. He switched the attentionseat to Peak Efficiency and a jolt of Quickpain brought him to Full Alert Status.

'To destroy every living creature on every world in every galaxy through the entire known universe and beyond.'

'Big job that, sir.'

'Exactly. Luckily, a Robot Telepath plant tipped us on how Sir Henry plans to accomplish his nefarious end. Brings us back to mibs. Fasterfaster has worked out a fiendishly simple Power Thrust which will set each star and planet in violent motion *towards one another*! Just imagine, if you will, a rough total of fourteen quadrillion-illion-million-zillion worlds hurled through space like immense marbles directly at each other!'

JamesTen whistled through his perfect teeth. 'And when they all make contact, sir?'

Z slapped a hand on the desk. 'End of the line for life as we know it today. The Big Casino. The Long Goodbye. The Final Blackout. The Ten Count. The Big Sleep. Curtains. Finis.'

'I believe I have the image, sir.'

Z paused to light a pseudokool. 'Now there's no reaching this chap with logic or sentiment. He must, in short, be snuffed out. That's your cup of tea, Ten. Chop-chop?'

'Chop-chop, sir.'

Z looked pleased. 'Well, then, you'll approach him as a Time Student. Tell him you want to go back to the Parallel Universe in which Rod Serling failed to sell *The Twilight Zone* to CBS, when *Peyton Place* and *The Beverly Hillbillies* couldn't find sponsors. You are to convince Sir Henry that you are researching a paper on Reverse Failure in Boffo Television.'

'I'll wear horn-rimmed glasses as a cover for my perfect eyes,' said JamesTen smugly.

'Then off you go, Ten. And I shall expect results. You JamesTen models take *ages* to replace!'

'Count on me, sir. I'll have the ugly brute's head on a plate within a fortnit'.'

'We haven't *got* a fortnit', confound you! I want him dead within twenty-four hours.'

'Done, sir. Am I free to disintegrate?'

'You are—and Godspeed, Ten! If you bring this one off, you save every living thing in creation. A job well worth the candle!'

JamesTen smiled thinly, saluted—and vanished in a shimmer of golden atoms.

The weathered, fog-dimmed sign on the Strand read:

TRAVEL BACK IN TIME AT LOW RATES! SEE LINCOLN LOSE A LOG-SPLITTING CONTEST! SEE HENRY FORD GO BROKE! SEE A FLAT-CHESTED MARILYN MONROE! SEE HANNIBAL GET LOST IN THE ALPS! COME IN NOW! FUN! EDUCATIONAL!

WINTER RATES! DON'T WAIT!

JamesTen, wearing tritoned Saturn Student Sneakers and a rakish Ruffalo pseudodacron UCLA Youth Shirt, adjusted his heavy pseudospecs and entered the shoddy plastic building housing E.T.T.T.P.U.

A grinning, cherub-faced gentleman nodded to him. The man was rosy-cheeked, fat and bearded. Only his coal-dark, bird-bright eyes betrayed his depravity. This, then, was Plugo Mittelholzer, alias Simon Brain, alias Kenneth Dankwardt, alias Socorro Quankenbush, alias Roman Belch, alias Clifford Siggfoos, alias—

'Yassssss?' the man hissed. 'Might I be of help?' There was no mistaking the odorous slime-soft hiss of a Neppie! JamesTen tightened his jaw.

'I wish a Time Trip,' he said. 'To the Irving Thalberg building at Metro. Located, I believe, just a wee bit below Venice Boulevard, in Culver City. Circa 1958.'

'That'll be thirteen thou. Credits. In advance. Got that much onya?'

'I believe that I have that sum upon my person,' nodded JamesTen. He reached casually for his thin leatherlife wallet which was actually not the smooth, fashion-tailored object it appeared to be, but was instead a deadly weapon which fired live centipedes. One bite from those poisoned fangs should do the trick.

However, before JamesTen could activate the firing pin, the wallet was judo-chopped from his hand, and he found himself staring into the cold pseudometal muzzle of a Neptunian blaster.

'Now, see here,' he protested, trying a shallow bluff, 'this is plain rudeness!'

'Let us end this nettlesome charade, Mr. JamesTen—android acting out of Greater New London on Her Majesty's Secret Service,' hissed Fasterfaster. 'Your identity is known to me. I had my Robot Telepath trail *your* Robot Telepath to HQ.'

'You damned fiend!'

Sir Henry laughed his snake's laugh.

'You came here pretending to want a trip in Time. And so you shall have it!'

Fasterfaster backed the agent into a tall, black box-like box.

'I'm sending you where you'll do me no further harm—

to a Yogurt Farm between Indio and Palm Springs, where you will be at the mercy of dedicated health addicts intent on slimming you down *their* way. Day and night you shall be fed only yogurt.'

JamesTen was horror-struck. 'But—but you *know* I cannot function without exotic, exquisitely prepared cuisine and rare, properly aged vintage wines brought to room temp. You *are* a fiend, Fasterfaster!'

'May your plastobones rot in the California desert! May buzzards pick your pseudoflesh!' hissed the master criminal —and threw a red plastic switch.

In a great spume of golden sparks, JamesTen and the Time Box vanished.

The android agent woke with a gonging headache. He was in a white room, on a white bed, covered by a white sheet.

'Are you okay now, mister?' asked a dulcet voice above him. 'Here, sip a little yogurt.'

JamesTen focused his eyes on a stunningly beautiful white girl standing beside the bed. Ah, he thought, so this is the one fatal flaw in Fasterfaster's thinking—to send me to a farm with *female* attendants!

'The only food I desire is the food of your lushly soft lips,' he said.

The girl dropped her yogurt. 'Golly, I—I ...'

JamesTen vaulted nakedly from the bed to catch her in his arms, crushing her softly lush body to his.

Exactly twelve minutes later, he was sprinting lithely across the desert towards the black boxlike box which stood, half-buried in sand, behind a clump of spiny dwarf cactus. His perfect love-making had forced the girl to reveal the area in which he had been discovered. Now it was only a simple matter of setting the time dials for Greater New London, circa the Present.

The box erupted into a tracery of golden atoms. JamesTen was on his way back to finish a very nasty job.

The tatty plastic building which housed E.T.T.T.P.U. was

empty when JamesTen stepped from the humming Time Box, gun at the ready. Sighing, he slipped the effective, handsomely ornamented Sheckley-Bernstein .20-40 double-charge weapon, equipped with Astro Silencer, back into its custom-worn pseudoalligator sheath holster in his left underarm cavity.

'Haven't got much time,' he reminded himself. Due to his having foolishly taken a short cut through a complex Space Warp, he'd actually used up twenty-three and one half of the twenty-four vital hours given him by Z. Another thirty minutes and the entire universe would cease to exist, and he'd have truly bungled the assignment.

Right at this moment, for all the android agent knew, Sir Henry Fasterfaster could be pseudosinging in some raw Opera dive on Mercury. Or he might be, even now, brazenly barrelhousing with a belly dancer from Barsoom. Or smugly riding as a passenger aboard a rusted Moon scow chugging through hyperspace for the Outer Dog Stars.

'Oh—frab!' JamesTen growled, relieving tension with the obscenity.

His perfect ears picked up a squeaking, rasping gasp from one corner of the room. He catstepped to the corner, gun at the ready.

'Mmm—M-mister J-James, sir . . . I . . . I . . .' It was an old Everett K. LXIII-Plus, the loyal-to-a-fault Robot Telepath working out of Z's office. He was a shocking tangle of broken wires, sprung cogs, and shorted circuits. One of his brown blue eyes rolled crazily in his square metal head.

'Can you talk, old chap?' asked JamesTen, bending over him. 'Where did Sir Henry go?'

Everett squeaked in pain. 'To . . . to . . .' The malfunctioning eye rattled to the floor and JamesTen kicked it aside irritably.

'Get to it, man! *Where!*'

'O-Off . . . ice . . . Z . . . Danger!'

'Great Scott! To Z's office. Why, he's out to harm the finest man the Service has ever known! And what of poor Miss Manypiggies? Why, that filthy—'

The dying robot gurgled metallically as the android agent rushed from the building.

Outside, in the thick soup of a Greater New London fog, JamesTen flagged down a Spacekab.

'Baker Street. 228. And make it chop-chop!' he snapped, handing the driver a thousandnote pre-punched credit.

'Cor blimey! Jus' you hold yer bloody hat, Gov, an' we's on our bloody way, we are! Hang on, yer Lordship!'

The kab lifted back into its prescribed airslot and rattled unsteadily towards Baker Street. JamesTen noted, with a certain degree of pleasure, that this kab was a vintage Nolag-Russeii model KXK-111 with the charmingly old-fashioned Intra-dish transmission aided by a fluted prefab twin-select overdrive.

'Pardon—but didn't this very model win the classic 24-Hour GP race for airkabs back at Le Mans in 1999?' he asked the driver.

'Cor, I dunno, yer Grace,' rasped the hairy little man. 'If you say so, she did! An' that's a fact!'

'I'm *certain* it was an N-R KXK job,' mused JamesTen. 'The twin-select unit funked out in the twenty-third hour, but ole Frabish-Suitgrave brought her over for the win. Great victory!' For a hushed moment, JamesTen was lost in the glory of past races—then he rallied with an oath. 'Why the frab aren't we getting there, man?'

'Bloody fog's got me 'arf crackers, Gov,' declared the hairy driver. 'I'm near off me nob, matie! Couldn't find me own arse in this stuff. An' that's a fact!'

'Take me down, then, you blundering fool, and I'll teleport in. That's what I should have done in the first place. Z will play merry hell with me if the universe goes up!'

The confused kabbie landed the KXK-111 atop a sagging plastic flower dispensary (featuring a sale on Venusian Tubers) and JamesTen scrambled to the ground, cursing the driver's oafish stupidity.

He found a teleport booth next door to an android marriage-counselling service—but two rat-haired old nannies were in line ahead of him.

'Stand aside,' he ordered crisply. 'I'm on Her Majesty's business.'

The first nannie grinned knowingly at her blowsy companion. 'My, my ... but ain't that what they *all* say, them what wants a decent woman's place in line.'

The second nannie cackled approval. 'Right ya are, Meg, dearie! Don't you budge an inch fer the cheeky sod!'

Nettled, JamesTen quickfired a double charge from his Sheckley-Bernstein into the two ladies. As they thumped heavily to the walk, he quickstepped over their smoking bodies into the booth.

Sir Henry Fasterfaster would indeed be surprised to see him!

Z's office was empty when the android agent appeared. Too late! Only five minutes left; then the universe was finished for good and all. And no Sir Henry.

'I've muddled the job,' sighed JamesTen, wearily holstering his .20-40.

'Indeed you have,' a voice hissed behind him. The agent catspun around on the balls of his perfect feet.

It was Z—emerging from a plastobroom closet with a service blaster held at belly-level.

'But, sir ... I—'

'The game is up,' Z grated, eyes alight with intense hatred.

'Great scott, sir, *you* must be—'

Of course, JamesTen told himself, Z was Fasterfaster! He'd been royally dupped by the master fiend! It all fell into place—or *did* it? Had Z sent him on a false hunt to clear the way for his—Fasterfaster's—inhuman scheme for mass destruction? If so, how long had Z been Fasterfaster? Or had there ever been a real Z? Or a real Fasterfaster? Perhaps Fasterfaster was now Z in disguise. Or was Z Fasterfaster all along? Or was ...? JamesTen's metal brain reeled in confusion.

The closet door opened again and Miss Manypiggies appeared, her eyes bright with hate. She held a blaster in her slender subtly tanned woman's hand, at tummy-level.

As Z's head swung towards her, JamesTen had his split-second chance. His perfect reflexes went into action and the efficient Sheckley-Bernstein .20-40 popped into his hand. He squeezed the pseudotrigger three times ... four ... five ... six ... seven ... eight ...

Z lay face down on the plastorug, reduced to a smoking mass.

JamesTen jauntily stowed his weapon. 'I'll wager *he* won't be destroying any universes, eh, Manypiggies?' He gave her his thin, smirking smile.

'He never intended to,' snapped the girl, 'but in just two minutes, *you* do!'

'What the deuce do you mean by that remark?'

'I mean—and please keep your gun hand by your side—that *you* are Sir Henry Fasterfaster!'

'Utter balderdash!' declared JamesTen with some heat. 'Wouldn't I bloody well know whether or not I was a master fiend?'

'Not in this particular case,' the girl replied, her tone level and cold. 'Among your many other evil arts, you are a master at self-hypnosis. You set up this inhuman plan for mass destruction and then—upon disguising yourself as an android agent—hypnotized yourself into believing you actually *were* one. The real JamesTen is dead. I found his body in there.' She indicated the closet. 'In just ten seconds, your hypnosis will wear off and you'll be Sir Henry again. Then you'll attempt to activate Operation Mibs.'

'But if I'm Sir Henry ... then who was the fat, rosy-cheeked, bewhiskered fellow who sent me to the Yogurt Farm at Indio?'

'A Robot Telepath programmed to impersonate your true evil self. Z had to believe you were JamesTen in order to ease off and give you, Sir Henry, a clear field. You knew he would not send out other agents if *he* knew JamesTen was on the job. And even his old loyal-to-a-fault Robot Telepath, Everett K. LXIII-Plus, could not penetrate your false identity, since your self-hypnotized mind offered no clue.'

'Then . . . then who did in old Everett?'

'The fat, rosy-cheeked, bewhiskered Robot Telepath—after you left for Indio.'

Miss Manypiggies briskly checked her pseudowatch. '*Now*—do you know who you really are?'

The android agent's perfect body dropped away like a cloak, revealing an ugly brute with a great long leathery neck, toad's eyes, distended red-rimmed nostrils, purple hands, immense kangaroo feet, and no teeth at all.

Sir Henry!

'I have one final question before we all dust away, my very clever Miss Maggie Manypiggies,' hissed the fiend. 'How did Z find out that I wasn't me? That is, that JamesTen was not JamesTen? Sorry I put that so awkwardly, but you follow what I'm asking, do you not?'

The girl nodded. 'When I discovered the real JamesTen's mutilated body in the closet, stuffed into the plastohamper, I told Z about it. It was just that simple. Leaving James in Z's closet was a stupid blunder.'

'No real harm done I'll wager,' hissed Sir Henry. 'When I press this red plastic button—' and he held up a long black tubelike tube with a crimson button on one end '—the entire universe will be reduced to ash, and I will be revenged for the cruel joke of my unnatural birth!'

At that precise instant, Miss Manypiggies fired.

Sir Henry Fasterfaster crumpled to the plastorug, knocking over a pseudolamp, the tube falling from his outflung purple hand. There was a long moment of silence.

What Miss Mannypiggies did not understand, what she absolutely could *not* fathom, was the fact that Sir Henry was now reduced to a mass of smoking wires and sprung cogs.

Which meant that he wasn't really . . .

Then, in that case, oh God! Could it possibly be that *she* was the real Sir Henry Fasterfaster?

Miss Manypiggies wisely decided not to think about that.

HE KILT IT WITH A STICK

A summer night in June.

Ellen away, visiting her parents. The house on Gillham Avenue empty, waiting.

Warm air.

A high, yellow moon.

Stars.

Crickets thrumming the dark.

Fireflies.

A summer night.

Fred goes to the Apollo to see a war film. It depresses him. All the killing. He leaves before it has ended, walking up the aisle and out of the deserted lobby and on past the empty glass ticket booth. Alone.

The sidewalk is bare of pedestrians.

It is late, near midnight, and traffic is very sparse. The wide street is silent. A truck grinds heavily away in the distance.

Fred begins to walk home.

He shouldn't. It is only two blocks: a few steps to the corner of 40th, then down the long hill to Gillham then right along to his house at the end of the block, near 41st. Not quite two blocks to walk. But too far for him. Too far.

Fred stops.

A grey cat is sleeping in the window of Rae's Drugstore. Fred presses the glass.

I could break the window—but that would be useless. The thing would be safe by then; it would leap away and I'd never find it in the store. The police would arrive and . . . No. Insane. Insane to think of killing it.

The grey cat, quite suddenly, opens its eyes to stare at Fred Baxter. Unblinking. Evil.

He shudders, moves quickly on.

The cat continues to stare.

Foul thing knows what I'd like to do to it.

The hill, sloping steeply, is tinted with cool moonlight. Fred walks down this hill, filled with an angry sense of frustration: he would very much have enjoyed killing the grey cat in the drugstore window.

Hard against chest wall, his heart judders. Once, twice, three times. Thud thud thud. He slows, removes a tissue-wrapped capsule from an inside pocket. Swallows the capsule. Continues to walk.

Fred reaches the bottom of the hill, crosses over.

Trees now. Big fat-trunked oaks and maples, fanning their leaves softly over the concrete sidewalk. Much darker. Thick tree-shadow midnight dark, broken by three street lamps down the long block. Lamps haloed by green night insects.

Deeper.

Into the summer dark....

When Fred Baxter was seven he wrote: 'Today a kitty cat bit me at school and it hurt a lot. The kitty was bad, so I kilt it with a stick.'

When he was ten, and living in St. Louis, a boy two houses up told Fred his parents wanted to get rid of a litter. 'I'll take care of it,' Fred assured him—and the next afternoon, in Miller Lake, he drowned all six of the kittens.

At fifteen, in high school, Fred trapped the janitor's Tabby in the gymnasium locker room, choked it to death, and carried it downstairs to the furnace. He was severely scratched in the process.

As a college freshman, Fred distributed several pieces of poisoned fish over the Rockhurst campus. The grotesquely twisted bodies of seven cats were found the next morning.

Working in the sales department of Hall Brothers, Fred was invited to visit his supervisor at home one Saturday—and was seen in the yard playing with Frances, a pet Siamese. She was later found crushed to death, and it was assumed a car had run over the animal. Fred quit his job ten days later because his supervisor had cat hands.

Fred married Ellen Ferber when he was thirty, and she wanted to have children right away. Fred said no, that babies were small and furry in their blankets, and disturbed him. Ellen bought herself a small kitten for company while Fred was on the road. He didn't object—but a week after the purchase, he took a meat knife and dismembered the kitten, telling Ellen that it had 'wandered away.' Then he bought her a green parakeet.

ZZZZZZZ Click

This is Frederick Baxter speaking and I ... wait, the sound level is wrong and I'll— There, it's all right now. I can't tell anyone about this—but today I found an old Tom in an alley downtown, and I got hold of the stinking, wretched animal and I ...

ZZZZZZZ Click

The heart trouble started when Fred was thirty-five.

'You have an unusual condition,' the doctor told him. 'You are, in effect, a medical oddity. Your chest houses a quivering-muscled heart—fibrillation. Your condition can easily prove fatal. Preventive measures must be taken. No severe exercise, no overeating, plenty of rest.'

Fred obeyed the man's orders—although he did not really trust a doctor whose cat eyes reflected the moon.

ZZZZZZZ Click

... awful time with the heart. Really awful. The use of digitalis drives me to alcohol, which sends my heart into massive flutters. Then the alcohol forces me into a need for more digitalis. It is a deadly circle and I ...

I have black dreams. A nap at noon and I dream of smothering. This comes from the heart condition. And because of the cats. They all fear me now, avoid me on the street. They've *told* one another about me. This is fact. Killing them is becoming quite difficult ... but I caught a big, evil one in the garden last Thursday and buried it. Alive. As

I am buried alive in these black dreams of mine. I got excited, burying the cat—and this is bad for me. I must go on killing them, but I must *not* get excited. I must stay calm and not—here comes Ellen, so I'd better ...

ZZZZZZZ Click

'What's wrong, Fred?'

It was 2 a.m. and Ellen had awakened to find him standing at the window.

'Something in the yard,' he said.

The moon was flushing the grass with pale gold—and a dark shape scuttled over the lawn, breaking the pattern. A cat shape.

'Go to sleep,' said his wife, settling into her pillow.

Fred Baxter stared at the cat, who stared back at him from the damp yard, its head raised, the yellow of the night moon now brimming the creature's eyes. The cat's mouth opened.

'It's sucking up the moonlight,' Fred whispered.

Then he went back to bed.

But he did not sleep.

Later, thinking about this, Fred recalled what his mother had often said about cats. 'They perch on the chest of a baby,' she'd said, 'place their red mouth over the soft mouth of the baby, and draw all the life from its body. I won't have one of the disgusting things in the house.'

Alone in the summer night, walking down Gillham Avenue, Fred passes a parked car, bulking black and silent in its gravel driveway. The closed car windows gleam deep yellow from the eyes inside.

Eyes?

Fred stops, looks back at the car.

It is packed with cats.

How many? Ten ... a dozen. More ... twenty, maybe. All inside the car, staring out at me. Dozens of foul, slitted yellow eyes.

Fred can do nothing. He checks all four doors of the silent automobile, finds them locked. The cats stare at him.

Filthy creatures!

He moves on.

The street is oddly silent. Fred realizes why: the crickets have stopped. No breeze stirs the trees; they hang over him, heavy and motionless in the summer dark.

The houses along Gillham are shuttered, lightless, closed against the night. Yet, on a porch, Fred detects movement.

Yellow eyes spark from porch blackness. A big, dark-furred cat is curled into a wooden swing. It regards Fred Baxter.

Kill it!

He moves with purposeful stealth, leans to grasp a stout tree limb which has fallen into the yard. He mounts the porch steps.

The dark-furred cat has not stirred.

Fred raises the heavy limb. The cat hisses, claws extended, fangs balefully revealed. It cries out like a wounded child and vanishes off the porch into the deep shadow between houses.

Missed. Missed the rotten thing.

Fred moves down the steps, crosses the yard towards the walk. His head is lowered in anger. When he looks up, the walk is thick with cats. He runs into them, kicking, flailing the tree club. They scatter, melting away from him like butter from a heated blade.

Thud thud thud. Fred drops the club. His heart is rapping, fisting his chest. He leans against a tree, sobbing for breath. The yellow-eyed cats watch him from the street, from bushes, from steps and porches and the tops of cars.

Didn't get a one of them. Not a damn one....

The fireflies have disappeared. The street lamps have dimmed to smoked circles above the heavy, cloaking trees. The clean summer sky is shut away from him—and Fred Baxter finds the air clogged with the sharp, suffocating smell of cat fur.

He walks on down the block.

The cats follow him.

He thinks of what fire could do to them—long blades of yellow crisping flame to flake them away into dark ash. But he cannot burn them; burning them would be impossible. There are *hundreds*. That many at least.

They fill driveways, cover porches, blanket yards, pad in lion-like silence along the street. The yellow moon is in their eyes, sucked from the sky. Fred, his terror rising, raises his head to look upward.

The trees are alive with them!

His throat closes. He cannot swallow. Cat fur cloaks his mouth.

Fred begins to run down the concrete sidewalk, stumbling, weaving, his chest filled with a terrible winged beating.

A sound.

The scream of the cats.

Fred claps both hands to his head to muffle the stab and thrust of sound.

The house ... must reach the house.

Fred staggers forward. The cat masses surge in behind him as he runs up the stone walk to his house.

A cat lands on his neck. Mutely, he flings it loose—plunges up the wooden porch steps.

Key. Find your key and unlock the door. Get inside!

Too late.

Eyes blazing, the cats flow up and over him, a dark, furry, stifling weight. As he pulls back the screen, claws and needle teeth rip at his back, arms, face, legs ... shred his clothing and skin. He twists wildly, beating at them. Blood runs into his eyes....

The door is open. He falls forward, through the opening. The cats swarm after him in hot waves, covering his chest, sucking the breath from his body. Baxter's thin scream is lost in the sharp, rising, all-engulfing cry of the cats.

A delivery boy found him two days later, lying face down

on the living-room floor. His clothes were wrinkled, but untorn.

A cat was licking the cold, white, unmarked skin of Frederick Baxter's cheek.

THE UNDERDWELLER

In the waiting, windless dark, Lewis Stillman pressed into the building-front shadows along Wilshire Boulevard. Breathing softly, the automatic poised and ready in his hand, he advanced with animal stealth towards Western Avenue, gliding over the night-cool concrete past ravaged clothing shops, drug and ten-cent stores, their windows shattered, their doors ajar and swinging. The city of Los Angeles, painted in cold moonlight, was an immense graveyard; the tall, white tombstone buildings thrust up from the silent pavement, shadow-carved and lonely. Overturned metal corpses of trucks, buses, and automobiles littered the streets.

He paused under the wide marquee of the Fox Wiltern. Above his head, rows of splintered display bulbs gaped—sharp glass teeth in wooden jaws. Lewis Stillman felt as though they might drop at any moment to pierce his body.

Four more blocks to cover. His destination: a small corner delicatessen four blocks south of Wilshire, on Western. Tonight he intended bypassing the larger stores like Safeway and Thriftimart, with their available supplies of exotic foods; a smaller grocery was far more likely to have what he needed. He was finding it more and more difficult to locate basic foodstuffs. In the big supermarkets, only the more exotic and highly spiced canned and bottled goods remained—and he was sick of caviare and oysters!

Crossing Western, as he almost reached the far kerb, he saw some of *them*. He dropped immediately to his knees behind the rusting bulk of an Oldsmobile. The rear door on his side was open, and he cautiously eased himself into the back seat of the deserted car. Releasing the safety catch on the automatic, he peered through the cracked window at six or seven of them, as they moved towards him along the street. God! Had he been seen? He couldn't be sure. Perhaps they were aware of his position! He should have remained on the open street, where he'd have a running chance. Perhaps, if his aim were true, he could kill most of them; but, even with its silencer, the gun might be heard and more of them would come. He dared not fire until he was certain they had discovered him.

They came closer, their small dark bodies crowding the walk, six of them, chattering, leaping, cruel mouths open, eyes glittering under the moon. Closer. Their shrill pipings increased, rose in volume. Closer. Now he could make out their sharp teeth and matted hair. Only a few feet from the car ... His hand was moist on the handle of the automatic; his heart thundered against his chest. Seconds away ...

Now!

Lewis Stillman fell heavily back against the dusty seat cushion, the gun loose in his trembling hand. They had passed by; they had missed him. Their thin pipings diminished, grew faint with distance.

The tomb silence of late night settled around him.

The delicatessen proved a real windfall. The shelves were relatively untouched and he had a wide choice of tinned goods. He found an empty cardboard box and hastily began to transfer the cans from the shelf nearest him.

A noise from behind—a padding, scraping sound.

Lewis Stillman whirled about, the automatic ready.

A huge mongrel dog faced him, growling deep in its throat, four legs braced for assault. The blunt ears were laid flat along the short-haired skull and a thin trickle of saliva seeped from the killing jaws. The beast's powerful chest muscles were bunched for the spring when Stillman acted.

His gun, he knew, was useless; the shots might be heard. Therefore, with the full strength of his left arm, he hurled a heavy can at the dog's head. The stunned animal staggered under the blow, legs buckling. Hurriedly, Stillman gathered his supplies and made his way back to the street.

How much longer can my luck hold? Lewis Stillman wondered, as he bolted the door. He placed the box of tinned goods on a wooden table and lit the tall lamp nearby. Its flickering orange glow illumined the narrow, low-ceilinged room.

Twice tonight, his mind told him, twice you've escaped them—and they could have seen you easily on both occasions if they had been watching for you. They don't know you're alive. But when they find out . . .

He forced his thoughts away from the scene in his mind, away from the horror; quickly he began to unload the box, placing the cans on a long shelf along the far side of the room.

He began to think of women, of a girl named Joan, and of how much he had loved her . . .

The world of Lewis Stillman was damp and lightless; it was narrow and its cold stone walls pressed in upon him as he moved. He had been walking for several hours; sometimes he would run, because he knew his leg muscles must be kept strong, but he was walking now, following the thin yellow beam of his hooded lantern. He was searching.

Tonight, he thought, I might find another like myself. Surely, *someone* is down here; I'll find someone if I keep searching. I *must* find someone!

But he knew he would not. He knew he would find only chill emptiness ahead of him in the long tunnels.

For three years, he had been searching for another man or woman down here in this world under the city. For three years, he had prowled the seven hundred miles of storm drains which threaded their way under the skin of Los Angeles like the veins in a giant's body—and he had found nothing. *Nothing.*

Even now, after all the days and nights of search, he could not really accept the fact that he was alone, that he was the last man alive in a city of seven million . . .

The beautiful woman stood silently above him. Her eyes burned softly in the darkness; her fine red lips were smiling. The foam-white gown she wore continually swirled and billowed around her motionless figure.

'Who are you?' he asked, his voice far off, unreal.

'Does it matter, Lewis?'

Her words, like four dropped stones in a quiet pool, stirred him, rippled down the length of his body.

'No,' he said. 'Nothing matters, now, except that we've found each other. God, after all these lonely months and years of waiting! I thought I was the last, that I'd never live to see—'

'Hush, my darling.' She leaned to kiss him. Her lips were moist and yielding. 'I'm here now.'

He reached up to touch her cheek, but already she was fading, blending into darkness. Crying out, he clawed desperately for her extended hand. But she was gone, and his fingers rested on a rough wall of damp concrete.

A swirl of milk-fog drifted away in slow rollings down the tunnel.

Rain. Days of rain. The drains had been designed to handle floods, so Lewis Stillman was not particularly worried. He had built high, a good three feet above the tunnel floor, and the water had never yet risen to this level. But he didn't like the sound of the rain down here: an orchestrated thunder through the tunnels, a trap-drumming amplified and continuous. Since he had been unable to make his daily runs, he had been reading more than usual. Short stories by Wolty, Gordimer, Aiken, Irwin Shaw, Hemingway; poems by Frost, Lorca, Sandburg, Millay, Dylan Thomas. Strange, how unreal this present day world seemed when he read their words. Unreality, however, was fleeting, and the moment he closed a book the loneliness and the fears pressed back. He hoped the rain would stop soon.

Dampness. Surrounding him, the cold walls and the chill and the dampness. The unending gurgle and drip of water, the hollow, tapping splash of the falling drops. Even in his cot, wrapped in thick blankets, the dampness seemed to permeate his body. Sounds ... Thin screams, pipings, chatterings, reedy whisperings above his head. They were dragging something along the street, something they'd killed, no doubt: an animal—a cat or a dog, perhaps ... Lewis Stillman shifted, pulling the blankets closer about his body. He kept his eyes tightly shut, listening to the sharp, scuffling sounds on the pavement, and swore bitterly.

'Damn you,' he said. 'Damn all of you!'

Lewis Stillman was running, running down the long tunnels. Behind him, a tide of midget shadows washed from wall to wall; high, keening cries, doubled and tripled by echoes, rang in his ears. Claws reached for him; he felt panting breath, like hot smoke, on the back of his neck. His lungs were bursting, his entire body aflame.

He looked down at his fast-pumping legs, doing their job with pistoned precision. He listened to the sharp slap of his heels against the floor of the tunnel, and he thought: I might die at any moment, but my *legs* will escape! They will run on, down the endless drains, and never be caught. They move so fast, while my heavy, awkward upper body rocks and sways above them, slowing them down, tiring them—making them angry. How my legs must hate me! I must be clever and humour them, beg them to take me along to safety. How well they run, how sleek and fine!

Then he felt himself coming apart. His legs were detaching themselves from his upper body. He cried out in horror, flailing the air, beseeching them not to leave him behind. But the legs cruelly continued to unfasten themselves. In a cold surge of terror, Lewis Stillman felt himself tipping, falling towards the damp floor—while his legs raced on with a wild animal life of their own. He opened his mouth, high above those insane legs, and screamed, ending the nightmare.

He sat up stiffly in his cot, gasping, drenched in sweat. He drew in a long, shuddering breath and reached for a cigarette, lighting it with a trembling hand.

The nightmares were getting worse. He realized that his mind was rebelling as he slept, spilling forth the bottled-up fears of the day during the night hours.

He thought once more about the beginning, six years ago—about why he was still alive. The alien ships had struck Earth suddenly, without warning. Their attack had been thorough and deadly. In a matter of hours, the aliens had accomplished their clever mission—and the men and women of Earth were destroyed. A few survived, he was certain. He had never seen any of them, but he was convinced they existed. Los Angeles was not the world, after all, and since he had escaped, so must have others around the globe. He'd been working alone in the drains when the aliens struck, finishing a special job for the construction company on B tunnel. He could still hear the weird sound of the mammoth ships and feel the intense heat of their passage.

Hunger had forced him out, and overnight he had become a curiosity. The last man alive. For three years, he was not harmed. He worked with them, taught them many things, and tried to win their confidence. But, eventually, certain ones came to hate him, to be jealous of his relationship with the others. Luckily, he had been able to escape to the drains. That was three years ago, and now they had forgotten him.

His subsequent excursions to the upper level of the city had been made under cover of darkness—and he never ventured out unless his food supply dwindled. He had built his one-room structure directly to the side of an overhead grating—not close enough to risk their seeing it, but close enough for light to seep in during the sunlight hours. He missed the warm feel of open sun on his body almost as much as he missed human companionship, but he dare not risk himself above the drains by day.

When the rain ceased, he crouched beneath the street gratings to absorb as much as possible of the filtered sunlight. But the rays were weak, and their small warmth only served to heighten his desire to feel direct sunlight upon his naked shoulders.

The dreams . . . always the dreams.

'Are you cold, Lewis?'

'Yes. Yes, cold.'

'Then go out, dearest. Into the sun.'

'I can't. Can't go out.'

'But Los Angeles is your world, Lewis! You are the last man in it. The last man in the world.'

'Yes, but they own it all. Every street belongs to them, every building. They wouldn't let me come out. I'd die. They'd kill me.'

'Go out, Lewis.' The liquid dream-voice faded, faded. 'Out into the sun, my darling. Don't be afraid.'

That night, he watched the moon through the street gratings for almost an hour. It was round and full, like a huge yellow floodlamp in the dark sky, and he thought, for the first time in years, of night baseball at Blues Stadium in Kansas City. He used to love watching the games with his father under the mammoth stadium lights when the field was like a pond, frosted with white illumination, and the players dream-spawned and unreal. Night baseball was always a magic game to him when he was a boy.

Sometimes he got insane thoughts. Sometimes, on a night like this, when the loneliness closed in like a crushing fist and he could no longer stand it, he would think of bringing one of them down with him, into the drains. One at a time, they might be handled. Then he'd remember their sharp, savage eyes, their animal ferocity, and he would realize that the idea was impossible. If one of their kind disappeared, suddenly and without trace, others would certainly become suspicious, begin to search for him—and it would all be over.

Lewis Stillman settled back into his pillow; he closed his eyes and tried not to listen to the distant screams, pipings, and reedy cries filtering down from the street above his head.

Finally, he slept.

He spent the afternoon with paper women. He lingered over the pages of some yellowed fashion magazines, looking at all the beautifully photographed models in their fine clothes. Slim and enchanting, these page-women, with their cool enticing eyes and perfect smiles, all grace and softness and glitter and swirled cloth. He touched their images with gentle fingers, stroking the tawny paper hair, as though, by some magic formula, he might imbue them with life. Yet, it was easy to imagine that these women had never *really* lived at all—that they were simply painted, in microscopic detail, by sly artists to give the illusion of photos.

He didn't like to think about these women and how they died.

'A toast to courage,' smiled Lewis Stillman, raising his wine glass high. It sparkled deep crimson in the lamplit room. 'To courage and to the man who truly possesses it!' He drained the glass and hastily refilled it from a tall bottle on the table beside his cot.

'Aren't you going to join me, Mr. H.?' he asked the seated figure slouched over the table, head on folded arms. 'Or must I drink alone?'

The figure did not reply.

'Well, then—' He emptied the glass, set it down. 'Oh, I know all about what one man is supposed to be able to do. Win out alone. Whip the damn world single-handed. If a fish as big as a mountain and as mean as all sin is out there, then this one man is supposed to go get him, isn't that it? Well, Papa H., what if the world is *full* of big fish? Can he win over them all? One man, alone? Of course he can't.

Nosir. Damn well right he can't!'

Stillman moved unsteadily to a shelf in one corner of the small wooden room and took down a slim book.

'Here she is, Mr. H. Your greatest. The one you wrote cleanest and best—*The Old Man and the Sea*. You showed how one man could fight the whole damn ocean.' He paused, voice strained and rising. 'Well, by God, show me, *now*, how to fight this ocean! My ocean is full of killer fish, and I'm one man and I'm alone in it. I'm ready to listen.'

The seated figure remained silent.

'Got you now, haven't I, Papa? No answer to this one, eh? Courage isn't enough. Man was not meant to live alone or fight alone—or drink alone. Even with courage, he can only do so much alone—and then it's useless. Well, I say it's useless. I say the hell with your book, and the hell with *you*!'

Lewis Stillman flung the book straight at the head of the motionless figure. The victim spilled back in the chair; his arms slipped off the table, hung swinging. They were lumpy and handless.

More and more, Lewis Stillman found his thoughts turning to the memory of his father and of long hikes through the moonlit Missouri countryside, of hunting trips and warm campfires, of the deep woods, rich and green in summer. He thought of his father's hopes for his future, and the words of that tall, grey-haired figure often came back to him.

'You'll be a fine doctor, Lewis. Study and work hard, and you'll succeed. I know you will.'

He remembered the long winter evenings of study at his father's great mahogany desk, poring over medical books and journals, taking notes, sifting and resifting facts. He remembered one set of books in particular—Erickson's monumental three-volume text on surgery, richly bound and stamped in gold. He had always loved those books, above all others.

What had gone wrong along the way? Somehow, the dream had faded; the bright goal vanished and was lost.

After a year of pre-med at the University of California, he had given up medicine; he had become discouraged and quit college to take a labourer's job with a construction company. How ironic that this move should have saved his life! He'd wanted to work with his hands, to sweat and labour with the muscles of his body. He'd wanted to earn enough to marry Joan and then, later perhaps, he would have returned to finish his courses. It seemed so far away now, his reason for quitting, for letting his father down.

Now, at this moment, an overwhelming desire gripped him, a desire to pore over Erickson's pages once again, to recreate, even for a brief moment, the comfort and happiness of his childhood.

He'd once seen a duplicate set on the second floor of Pickwick's bookstore in Hollywood, in their used book department, and now he knew he must go after it, bring the books back with him to the drains. It was a dangerous and foolish desire, but he knew he would obey it. Despite the risk of death, he would go after the books tonight. *Tonight.*

One corner of Lewis Stillman's room was reserved for weapons. His prize, a Thompson submachine gun, had been procured from the Los Angeles police arsenal. Supplementing the Thompson were two automatic rifles, a Lüger, a Colt .45, and a .22 calibre Hornet pistol equipped with a silencer. He always kept the smallest gun in a spring-clip holster beneath his armpit, but it was not his habit to carry any of the larger weapons with him into the city. On this night, however, things were different.

The drains ended two miles short of Hollywood—which meant he would be forced to cover a long and particularly hazardous stretch of ground in order to reach the bookstore. He therefore decided to take along the .30 calibre Savage rifle in addition to the small hand weapon.

You're a fool, Lewis, he told himself as he slid the oiled Savage from its leather case, risking your life for a set of books. Are they *that* important? Yes, a part of him replied, they are that important. You want these books, then go *after* what you want. If fear keeps you from seeking that which you truly want, if fear holds you like a rat in the dark, then you are worse than a coward. You are a traitor, betraying yourself and the civilization you represent. If a man wants a thing and the thing is good, he must go after it, no matter what the cost, or relinquish the right to be called a man. It is better to die with courage than to live with cowardice.

Ah, Papa Hemingway, breathed Stillman, smiling at his own thoughts. I see that you are back with me. I see that your words have rubbed off after all. Well, then, all right—let us go after our fish, let us seek him out. Perhaps the ocean will be calm . . .

Slinging the heavy rifle over one shoulder, Lewis Stillman set off down the tunnels.

Running in the chill night wind. Grass, now pavement, now grass beneath his feet. Ducking into shadows, moving stealthily past shops and theatres, rushing under the cold, high moon. Santa Monica Boulevard, then Highland, then Hollywood Boulevard, and finally—after an eternity of heartbeats—Pickwick's.

Lewis Stillman, his rifle over one shoulder, the small automatic gleaming in his hand, edged silently into the store.

A paper battleground met his eyes.

In filtered moonlight, a white blanket of broken-backed volumes spilled across the entire lower floor. Stillman shuddered; he could envision them, shrieking, scrabbling at the shelves, throwing books wildly across the room at one another. Screaming, ripping, destroying.

What of the other floors? *What of the medical section?*

He crossed to the stairs, spilled pages crackling like a fall of dry autumn leaves under his step, and sprinted up the first short flight to the mezzanine. Similar chaos!

He hurried up to the second floor, stumbling, terribly afraid of what he might find. Reaching the top, heart thudding, he squinted into the dimness.

The books were undisturbed. Apparently they had tired

of their game before reaching these.

He slipped the rifle from his shoulder and placed it near the stairs. Dust lay thick all around him, powdering up and swirling as he moved down the narrow aisles; a damp, leathery mustiness lived in the air, an odour of mould and neglect.

Lewis Stillman paused before a dim, hand-lettered sign: MEDICAL SECTION. It was just as he remembered it. Holstering the small automatic, he struck a match, shading the flame with a cupped hand as he moved it along the rows of faded titles. Carter ... Davidson ... Enright ... *Erickson*. He drew in his breath sharply. All three volumes, their gold stamping dust-dulled but legible, stood in tall and perfect order on the shelf.

In the darkness, Lewis Stillman carefully removed each volume, blowing it free of dust. At last, all three books were clean and solid in his hands.

Well, you've done it. You've reached the books and now they belong to you.

He smiled, thinking of the moment when he would be able to sit down at the table with his treasure and linger again over the wondrous pages.

He found an empty carton at the rear of the store and placed the books inside. Returning to the stairs, he shouldered the rifle and began his descent to the lower floor.

So far, he told himself, my luck is still holding.

But as Lewis Stillman's foot touched the final stair, his luck ran out.

The entire lower floor was alive with them!

Rustling like a mass of giant insects, gliding towards him, eyes gleaming in the half-light, they converged upon the stairs. They'd been waiting for him.

Now, suddenly the books no longer mattered. Now only his life mattered and nothing else. He moved back against the hard wood of the stair-rail, the carton of books sliding from his hands. They had stopped at the foot of the stairs; they were silent. looking up at him with hate in their eyes.

If you can reach the street, Stillman told himself, then

you've still got half a chance. That means you've got to get through them to the door. All right then, *move*.

Lewis Stillman squeezed the trigger of the automatic. Two of them fell as Stillman rushed into their midst.

He felt sharp nails claw at his shirt, heard the cloth ripping away in their grasp. He kept firing the small automatic into them, and three more dropped under his bullets, shrieking in pain and surprise. The others spilled back, screaming, from the door.

The pistol was empty. He tossed it away, swinging the heavy Savage free from his shoulder as he reached the street. The night air, crisp and cool in his lungs, gave him instant hope.

I can still make it, thought Stillman, as he leaped the kerb and plunged across the pavement. If those shots weren't heard, then I've still got the edge. My legs are strong; I can outdistance them.

Luck, however, had failed him completely on this night. Near the intersection of Hollywood Boulevard and Highland, a fresh pack of them swarmed towards him.

He dropped to one knee and fired into their ranks, the Savage jerking in his hands. They scattered to either side.

He began to run steadily down the middle of Hollywood Boulevard, using the butt of the heavy rifle like a battering ram as they came at him. As he neared Highland, three of them darted directly into his path. Stillman fired. One doubled over, lurching crazily into a jagged plate glass store front. Another clawed at him as he swept around the corner to Highland, but he managed to shake free.

The street ahead of him was clear. Now his superior leg power would count heavily in his favour. Two miles. Could he make it before others cut him off?

Running, reloading, firing. Sweat soaking his shirt, rivering down his face, stinging his eyes. A mile covered. Halfway to the drains. They had fallen back behind his swift stride.

But more of them were coming, drawn by the rifle shots, pouring in from side streets, from stores and houses.

His heart jarred in his body, his breath was ragged. How many of them around him? A hundred? Two hundred? More coming. God!

He bit down on his lower lip until the salt taste of blood was on his tongue. You can't make it, a voice inside him shouted. They'll have you in another block and you know it!

He fitted the rifle to his shoulder, adjusted his aim, and fired. The long rolling crack of the big weapon filled the night. Again and again he fired, the butt jerking into the flesh of his shoulder, the bitter smell of burnt powder in his nostrils.

It was no use. Too many of them. He could not clear a path.

Lewis Stillman knew that he was going to die.

The rifle was empty at last; the final bullet had been fired. He had no place to run because they were all around him, in a slowly closing circle.

He looked at the ring of small cruel faces and thought, The aliens did their job perfectly; they stopped Earth before she could reach the age of the rocket, before she could threaten planets beyond her own moon. What an immensely clever plan it had been! To destroy every human being on Earth above the age of six—and then to leave as quickly as they had come, allowing our civilization to continue on a primitive level, knowing that Earth's back had been broken, that her survivors would revert to savagery as they grew into adulthood.

Lewis Stillman dropped the empty rifle at his feet and threw out his hands. 'Listen,' he pleaded, 'I'm really one of you. You'll *all* be like me soon. Please, *listen* to me.'

But the circle tightened relentlessly around him.

Lewis Stillman was screaming when the children closed in.

SOLUTION

He entered the dim chamber, pausing just inside, his back pressed against the door. In the soft semi-darkness the room smelled of iron and aluminium and brass. Ahead of him, dials glowed faintly. Lord, but this is fine, he thought, breathing deeply, hands clenched. He closed his eyes in the warm familiar dark, thinking, This is where I belong; here I am complete.

Norman Jerome Hollander, Servant of the Ship.

He opened his eyes, pupils adjusting to the dimness. Across the length of the chamber, a rising wall of tiny multi-coloured lights winked and gleamed. Needles steadied at correct pressure levels; round dial faces hummed softly, regulating the vast power of the Ship, guiding it through space towards—

Norman Hollander swore, knuckling his forehead with a clenched fist. He didn't want to think about the Ship's destination. It seemed so grossly unfair. But that was how it must seem to all the Servants at such a time. Each thinking the same sad thoughts, each cursing the impersonal machine which had passed its irrevocable judgment.

He moved slowly towards the glowing panel and lowered himself into the cushioning depth of the control chair. Around him he savoured the immense breathing presence of the Ship, its muted atomics, deep-buried in their ribbed and layered metal tons, sending out an almost imperceptible vibration which trembled along each nerve and muscle of Norman Hollander's body. In front of him, dials whirred, wheels spun, clicked; wires sang. The Ship was alive, but he was no longer a part of her life. He was now simply a passenger on the way to a destination he hated to reach.

Hollander sighed, removing the slotted metal card from his uniform pocket. He didn't need any light to read the words; they were graven on his brain. He would always remember them:

OUTCOME OF TEST LI76X: June 29, 2163
OPERATIONAL STATUS: NEGATIVE

The silver needles had entered his veins. Electronic devices had measured his heartbeat, his hearing, his blood pressure. His reaction time was checked, his entire body combed for the slightest imperfection. And, finally, that imperfection had been found, the verdict rendered. Negative. The one word he'd been dreading, the one word which meant that his job was over, that he was no longer a part of the Ship, could no longer serve her. For eighty-five years, while she hovered in space, suspended above alien planets, mining the rich ores from a thousand strange worlds, Norman Hollander had lovingly guided her efforts. His human hand had moved her delicate metal spider-hands which probed the surfaces of those far-flung worlds for storable riches. She was a Hundred Year Ship, designed and built to remain in space for ten full decades while her great storage compartments were gradually filled. Then, and only then, would she come home. Unless ...

Unless her Servant fails a test, thought Norman Hollander. Unless she finds her Servant wanting, imperfect. Then she rejects him, takes him back to Earth.

Hollander was 105, barely middle-aged by current Earth standards, but old for space. Ideally, though, he should have been able to remain with the Ship for those last fifteen precious years. But human weakness had cheated him of this. Hollander leaned forward, peering at his own reflection in the circular dial to his right. Not an old face. A strong face, marked with duty, but not old. Science had kept him young—but even the wonders of science could not make him perfect, as the Ship was perfect. And so she was taking him home.

No, not home, he thought bitterly. My home is here, with the Ship; I was born and bred for this and nothing else. Earth is simply a place, faintly-remembered, which I'll reach in forty-eight hours—after all these years as strange as any world I've ever visited. No, not home.

'When is he due?' asked Dr. Burack.

His assistant, David Miller, placed the schedule on Burack's desk. 'Tomorrow morning,' Miller said.

Burack looked at the schedule. Then he met Miller's cool gaze. 'I hope we have some luck with this one,' he said. 'Are your men posted?'

Miller nodded. 'He'll be observed from the moment the Ship touches down. Personally, I'm not optimistic. The pattern seems fixed.'

Dr. Burack tapped one finger gently against the schedule. 'Patterns can be broken. That's the biggest part of our job. I want the usual hourly report on Hollander. We've got a lot to learn yet, but we may be getting closer to a solution. This time David, we *may* win.'

'I wouldn't count on it sir,' said David Miller.

Lying on his side in the bed, Hollander stared out at the stars pricking the dark night sky beyond his window. The stars were telling him that he should be up there with them, that he had no business on this world called Earth. The stars understood him. No one here, on this stifling planet, understood him. No one.

Oh, they'd tried to make him feel at home. He was given this modern house, equipped with every electronic comfort; the latest Jetcar waited in the garage; a full wardrobe of clothes had been provided—all gifts for his service from a grateful government. They gave him everything except the chance to go back.

His family also tried. They had done all they possibly could to assure him that he was wanted, welcome, that he was now a part of their society once again, that he *belonged*. Yet his parents were strangers to him. He'd been a boy of seventeen when he'd seen them last; now they were smiling, friendly strangers, and he found nothing of himself in them.

From the moment his feet touched Earth he had begun to hate.

He hated the crowds shouting at him; he hated this house, the car, the clothes ... He even found himself hating his mother and father. They were part of the society which had taken him from space. He felt trapped and betrayed by all these smiling people, the men and women who shook his hand, who told him how heroic he was, how noble he had been, serving alone 'out there' for all those years. They gave him medals; they made speeches about him and, through it all, he wanted to damn them, to loose his hatred for what they had done to him.

Hollander often wondered about the Servants who had landed before him. Dozens of them, at the very least. Yet no one seemed to know anything about them; no records existed to prove that any of them had ever come back. Was he, in fact, the only man to have survived the Ships? When he asked questions about other Servants his inquiries were shrugged aside. No, they told him, there were no others. He had questioned his parents, but they said they knew nothing about the Servants. In their denials, however, Hollander had detected a guilt, an uneasiness.

The first month had been hell.

Five days after his homecoming he'd knocked down a man in the street. The man had made an insulting remark about the Ships and those who served them. He could still hear the fellow's mocking voice: '*You have to be insane to stay out there all that time on those damned tubs. You have to be crazy to do a thing like that!*' And Norman Hollander had knocked him to the street. If he hadn't been pulled away he might have throttled the man.

The fool! Hollander could feel the angry heat rising in his body.

During the second week he'd gone to the Psyc Centre and allowed the machines to put him through analysis. Adjust, they advised him. Learn to adjust to your society. But Norman Hollander had rejected them, as their Ship had rejected him.

In the third week he had attacked a Lawman. Only his status as a retired Servant had kept him from severe punishment.

I had my reasons, Hollander recalled. When I asked him

why there were no other Servants he had smiled like some kind of sly cat—and I wanted to smash that smile, destroy it.

And last week; that had been the worst. He drank for an entire morning, then took out the car. The afternoon ended in near-disaster when a schoolgirl had crossed the traffic strip ahead of him and he hadn't seen her. In avoiding her, he crashed. They took the car away from him. From *him*, the man whose hands had guided the great Ship!

What next? Hollander asked himself, what will I do next? I can never accept this exile, this living death. If they keep me here I'll end up killing somebody. Anybody. They're *all* to blame.

Sighing wearily, he closed his eyes, shutting out the bright, beckoning stars ...

'He isn't responding,' said David Miller. 'He's like the others. And we've done everything.'

Dr. Burack put aside the folder marked HOLLANDER and stood up. He walked past his assistant to the window. Ninety storeys below traffic moved swiftly along the jet strips.

'I've called him in,' Burack said, the tone of defeat evident in his voice. 'He knows that he can't go back into space. But he also knows that he's a freak here in our world. That's the price a Servant pays. Abnormality is a virtue with the Ships; a normal man would be useless to us. Perhaps, some day, we can reverse the pattern. But not yet. Not now.'

'Then you're going to commit him?' asked Miller.

'What else can I do at this point? If I don't commit him he'll break, turn violent. Hollander's a potential killer.'

'He's also a public hero.'

Burack smiled without warmth. 'So were all the others. At least the public is well aware of our problem. That's why they built the Servants' Institution. Here the Hollanders can find peace. They won't find it anywhere else on Earth.'

Miller nodded. 'Maybe we can save the next one,' he

said. 'We're advancing with each case. Maybe, next time, the Ships won't win.'

Dr. Burack said nothing. He continued to stare at the distant ribbons of traffic.

Hollander walked down the long, brilliantly-illumined corridor, arms swinging loosely at his sides, his fingertips brushing the regulation stripe on his trousers. It was wonderful to be wearing his uniform again, and the close-fitting jacket gave him a sense of security he hadn't felt since the landing. He enjoyed the echoing slap of his boots against the smooth marble floor. Yes, it was good of them to give him back his uniform.

'Here we are, Norman,' said Dr. Burack, indicating a heavy door. 'This is where you'll stay from now on. I think you'll find we've thought of everything.'

'Thank you,' said Hollander. 'I'm sure you have.'

The two men shook hands.

'Goodbye, Doctor.'

'Goodbye, Norman.'

Dr. Burack watched Hollander go into the special room. He drew a long breath, then turned away.

He entered the dim chamber, pausing just inside, his back pressed against the door. In the soft, semi-darkness the room smelled of iron and aluminium and brass. Ahead of him, dials glowed faintly. Lord, but this is fine, he thought, breathing deeply, hands clenched. He closed his eyes in the warm familiar dark, thinking, This is where I belong; here I am complete:

Norman Jerome Hollander, Servant of the Ship.

Clayton Weber eased himself down from the papier mâché mountain and wiped the artificial sweat from his face. 'How'd I look?' he asked the director.

'Great,' said Victor Raddish. 'Even Morell's own mother wouldn't know the difference.'

'That's what I like to hear,' grinned Weber, seating himself at a makeup table. Thus far, *Courage at Cougar Canyon,* starring 'fearless' Claude Morell as the Yellowstone Kid had gone smoothly. Doubling for Morell, Weber had leaped chasms, been tossed from rolling wagons, dived into rivers and otherwise subjected himself to the usual rigours of a movie stuntman. Now, as he removed his makeup, he felt a hand at his shoulder.

'Mr Morell would like to see you in his dressing room,' a studio messenger boy told him.

Inside the small room Weber lit a cigarette and settled back on the brown leather couch. Claude Morell, tall and frowning, stood facing him.

'Weber, you're a nosy, rotten bastard and I ought to have you thrown off the lot and blacklisted with every studio in town.'

'Then Linda told you about my call?'

'Of course she did. Your imitation of my voice was quite excellent. Seems you do as well off-camera as on. She was certain that *I* was talking or she never would have—'

'—discussed the abortion,' finished Weber, feet propped on the couch.

Morell's eyes hardened. 'How much do you want to keep silent?' Morell seated himself at a dressing table and flipped open his chequebook.

'Bribery won't be necessary,' smiled Clayton Weber through the spiralling smoke of his cigarette. 'I don't intend to spill the beans to Hedda Hopper. The fact that you impregnated the star of our picture and that she is about to have an abortion will never become public knowledge. You can depend on that.'

Morell looked confused. 'Then ... I don't—'

'Have you ever heard of the parallel universe theory?'

Morell shook his head, still puzzled.

'It's simply this—that next to our own universe an infinite number of parallel universes exist—countless millions of them—each in many ways identical to this one. Yet the life pattern is different in each. Every variation of living is carried out, with a separate universe for each variation. Do you follow me?'

Obviously, Morell did not.

'Let me cite examples,' said Weber. 'In one of these parallel universes Lincoln was never assassinated; in another Columbus did *not* discover America, nor did Joe Louis become heavyweight champ. In one universe America *lost* the First World War ...'

'But that's ridiculous,' Morell said. 'Dream stuff.'

'Let me approach it from another angle,' persisted Weber. 'You've heard of Doppelgangers?'

'You mean—*doubles?*'

'Not simply doubles, they are exact duplicates.' Weber drew on his cigarette, allowing his words to take effect. 'The reason you never see two of them together, for comparison, is that one of them always knows he is a duplicate of the other—and stays out of the other's life. Or enters it wearing a disguise.'

'You're talking gibberish,' said Claude Morell.

'Bear with me. The true Doppelganger *knows* he is not of this universe—and he chooses to stay away from his duplicate because it is too painful for him to see his own life being lived by another man, to see his wife and children and know they can never be his. So he builds a new life for himself in another part of the world.'

'I don't see the point, Weber. What are you telling me?'

Clayton Weber smiled. 'You'll see my point soon enough.' He continued. 'Sometimes a man or woman will simply vanish, wink out, as it were without a trace. Ambrose Bierce, the writer, was one of these. Then there was the crew of the *Marie Celeste* ... They unknowingly reached a point in time and space that allowed them to step through into a separate world, like and yet totally unlike their own. They became Doppelgangers.'

Weber paused, his eyes intent on Morell. '*I'm* one of them,' he said. 'It happened to me as it happened to them, without any warning. One moment I was happily married with a beautiful wife and a baby girl—the next I found myself in the middle of Los Angeles. Sometimes it's impossible to adjust to the situation. Some of us end up in an institution, claiming we're other people.' He smiled again. 'And—of course we *are*.'

Morell stood up, replacing the chequebook in his coat. 'I don't know what kind of word game you're playing, Weber, but I've had enough of it. You refuse my offer—all right, you're fired. And if a word of this affair with Linda Miller ever hits print I'll not only see that you never work again in the industry, I'll also see you receive the beating of your life. And I have the connections to guarantee a *thorough* job.'

'Do one thing for me, Mr Morell,' asked Weber. 'Just hold out your right hand, palm up.'

'I don't see—'

'Please.'

Morell brought up his hand. Weber raised his own, placing it beside Morell's. 'Look at them,' he said. 'Look at the shape of the thumbs, the lines in the palm, the whorls on each finger-tip.'

'Good God!' said Claude Morell.

The man who called himself Clayton Weber reached up and began to work on his face. The cheek lines were altered as he withdrew some inner padding, his nose became smaller as he peeled away a thin layer of wax. In a moment the change was complete.

'Incredible,' Morell breathed. 'That's my face!'

'I had to look enough like you to get this job as your

double,' Weber told him, 'but of course I couldn't look *exactly* like you. Now, however, we are identical.' He withdrew the Colt from the hip holster of his western costume and aimed it at Morell.

'No blanks this time,' he said.

'But why kill me?' Morell backed to the wall. 'Even if all you said is true, why kill me? They'll send you to the gas chamber. You'll die with me!'

'Wrong,' grinned Weber. 'The death will be listed as a suicide. A note will be found on the dresser in the apartment I rented, stating "Clayton Weber's" intention to do away with himself, that he felt he'd always been a failure, nothing but a stuntman, while others became stars. It will make excellent sense to the police. I will report that you shot yourself in my presence as we discussed the career you could never have.'

'But my face will be the face of Claude Morell, not Clayton Weber!'

'Half of your face will be disposed of by the bullet at such close range. There will be no question of identity. And we're both wearing the same costume.'

Morell leaned forward, eyes desperate. 'But why? Why?'

'I'm killing you for what you did to my wife,' said Weber, holding the gun steady.

'But—I never *met* your wife.'

'In your world, this world, Linda Miller was just another number on your sexual hit parade, but in my world she was my wife. In *my* world that baby girl she carries in her body was born, allowed to live. And that's just the way it's going to happen now. If you'd married Linda I would have disappeared, gone to live in another city, left you alone. But you didn't. So, *I'll* marry her—again.'

Claude Morell chose that moment to spring for the gun, but the bullet from the big Colt sent his head flying into bright red pieces.

The man who had called himself Clayton Weber placed the smoking weapon in Morell's dead hand.

Plippity-plop.

A girl a night.

Rainbow chicks: blonde on Monday, brunette on Tuesday, redhead on Wednesday. Falling like soft, ripe plums into Des Cahill's bed. Des shook the tree, and down they came.

Plippity-plop.

Ole Des, the Makeout King. Cahill the Cool. Mr. Codpiece. Remember how it was? Every young stud in the country envied him—walked like Des in his Gucci buckle-clips, wore his hair with the same cruel curl over one eye, thumb-crushed his cigs after three quick puffs the same savage way Des did?

Sure. Who could forget?

But now he's gone. No more movies or TV specials or Broadway guest shots in the nude. Women (and a lot of men) paid scalpers up to a hundred bucks to get a front-row peek at Cahill's equipment, and they were never disappointed.

So what happened? How come, at the top of the ladder, he walks, does the big fade, and is seen no more? I can tell you. I figure his public deserves to have the real rap laid down on Des Cahill.

I was his best friend—if he ever had one. My name is Albert. I took care of his income tax problems and lent him my shoulder. For crying on. And believe me, Des had plenty to cry about.

It begins with a ghost.

Des liked to swing high. His pad was in Benedict Canyon. Rafters, crackling fire, mile-deep rugs, a bear's head on the wall. Cosy. I was working in the back of the house, late one night, on a capital gains tax dodge for Des—my first time over to his place—when I hear this agonized female shriek of fear from the master bedroom. As I rush towards the room, out the door comes this pneumatic blonde wearing Midnight Hush eye make-up and a really terrified expression. She snake-shakes into her clothes, looking great doing it, and does a quick exit. Then she misses three gears on her MG going down the hill.

Des is standing by the bed, wearing a rumpled pair of Tiger's Eye shorts and looking bereft. That's the only word for how he looked. Bereft.

'It was him again,' he says softly.

'Who's him?'

'The frigging ghost. Who the hell else would I have in there?'

Right away, I take his word.

'Then you've seen this spook before?'

At my question, Des chuckles. He laughs. He throws back his head and howls. He falls down on the rug, breaking up. Then he stops and looks at me.

'Albert,' he says, 'I am going to tell you something I have never told anybody else in this living world. I'm twenty-five, loaded with bread, up to my ass in fame, with maybe ten thousand cuddly little numbers ready to make the sex scene any time I lift a pinky—and you know what?'

'What?'

'Albert, I am a virgin.'

We have a drink. Two drinks. We're on our third (vodka martinis with hair on their chests) when Des lays it out for me.

'First time I tried to make it all the way with a chick, I was fifteen—and that's when I saw him. The ghost. In broad daylight, at the beach on a Saturday afternoon. An old geezer dressed in full armour, looming right above us with this horse over his head.'

I stop Des there and he tells me that whenever the ghost appears, he is always holding up a horse—holding it in the air.

'Like he's about to throw it at you,' says Des. 'Anyhow, the chick fainted and I was very disturbed. It happened again the following Friday, with me and the mayor's daughter. And that's the way it's been ever since. I get a chick into the hay and we are at the absolute moment of truth, you know . . .'

'I know.'

'. . . and *that's* when the ghost comes on with the horse. Naturally, it scares the shit out of my date.'

'Naturally.'

'No matter where I am, it happens. On location down in Pennsylvania last summer for the coal mine flick, I had every precious young available female in town panting at my motel door. So I took 'em on, one per night, and always got up to the grand moment, you know . . .'

'I know.'

'. . . when out he pops with his goddamn overhead horse, and the scene is blown. Thirty-six days on location, thirty-six chicks, thirty-six blowups.' He knuckles his eyes, rolls his head. 'Albert, I cannot go on. I've got the hottest sex rep in show biz, and I haven't made it once.' He sobs—a broken, terrible sound. 'Not *once*!'

That's when I give him my shoulder.

To cry on.

Later, I give him advice. Hire a class ghost-breaker, who knows his spooks, and go after the bastard with the horse.

This he does. The ghost-breaker is a nervous, kinky little guy, but he guarantees his work. There will no longer be a ghost when he is through. This we can bank on.

He goes the full route. With powders that flash and explode. With chalked circles around the bed and invocations and curses and lots of arm-waving. With incense that really stinks and hand-clapping and plenty of yelling.

But each time, just as Des and the particular lady of his choice reach the ultimate moment, WHAP! the ghost is there. Naturally, all the stinking incense and exploding powders and yelling and hand-clapping don't exactly delight the young thing who happens to be sharing the sheets with Des, and she always demands to know just what the hell is going on with this creepy guy hopping nervously around their bed. But Des is able to calm her down, and she's usually okay until the ghost shows. At which point she bolts, like they all bolt—straight out of the room, shrieking.

This goes on for three weeks, with Des getting thinner and more bereft-looking by the week. Finally, I ask him if he'd mind if I joined the group—to kind of size up the ghost for myself and maybe come in with some fresh ideas. Sure, he says, and that night there's Des and the uneasy ghost-breaker and a redhead with an immense heaving bosom and me, all of us in the master bedroom.

Sex, under these conditions, is never good—but Des manages to thrash himself in to a damned remarkable performance until, ZAMBO! there's the ghost, right on the ole button.

I give him the careful once-over. A seedy old gink, scowling inside a cheapsie suit of backlot armour, with a crazy-eyed palomino above his head. I concentrate on the face. Suddenly, I let out a whoop.

'I *know* the bum! That's Joey Gibbler. It's Gibbler, I tell you!'

The ghost looks startled and vanishes, but, by then, the girl is shrieking and the nervous ghost-breaker is exploding more powders and Des is in no real condition to listen to me.

After, when things are more settled, I spell it out.

'Gibbler was an extra back in the days of the silents,' I tell Des. 'I remember reading about how he and this palomino horse both broke their necks doing a battle sequence for *The Queen's Cute Question*, one of those slapstick historicals they used to grind out at Monarch.'

Des shoots up an eyebrow. 'Dad directed that one—I know he did. It was his last picture.'

'Exactly! And he died of a stroke the following week. Which explains everything.'

'Not to me, it doesn't.'

'Joey was sore over getting his neck broke, and he blamed your pop for it. But he didn't have time to haunt him. The stroke beat him out. So Gibbler decides to haunt *you* instead. He waits until you're old enough to taste the sweet fruits of life and then he cunningly denies them to you. And he'll keep on until we placate him.'

'But how? How do you placate a sore spook?'

'The key is Joey Gibbler, Jr. The kid must be about thirty by now. Not bad-looking, I've seen his name in the trades.'

'An extra trying to make it as an actor?'

'Right. So set it up for him. Throw around some weight at the studio and get him into a picture. Junior clicks, and his old man stops haunting you out of sheer gratitude. You can do it.'

'Albert,' he says, 'I can do it.'

He does it. Joey winds up with a fat part in *The Big Bottom* and overnight, the way it can happen, Joey Gibbler, Jr. is a star.

And, overnight, Des makes it all the way through the moment of truth. No ghost. Ole Des Cahill is devirginized.

He hugs me, dances me around the room, thrusts signed cheques at me, insists that I accept his mother's wedding ring. It is a tearful, joyous occasion.

The next night, I get a jingle at my place. Des on the horn. Sounding terribly bereft.

'What's wrong?' I ask.

'A new one showed,' he says.

'Another ghost?'

'Albert, it can't be—but it is. It's Joey Jr.'

I buzz over to Benedict Canyon in my Porsche. Des meets me at the door, crazy-eyed like the palomino.

We get it all on the eleven o'clock news: 'Actor dies in freak set accident. Rising star Joey Gibbler, Jr. suffers a broken neck when a delicatessen set falls on him during a Jewish film sequence.' Wow.

Des sighs. 'That accounts for the white butcher's apron he's wearing and what he holds above his head.'

'Which is?'

'A display case full of, mostly, bagels and cream cheese.'

I'm sorry to tell you, but this story has no happy ending. Des, who swears he'll never resign himself to celibacy, has quit the acting game and is on the move. Last I heard, he'd covered most of Europe, Asia, and the Middle East, and was in the Australian back country.

What he's looking for is a very brave chick, well-stacked, eighteen to twenty-five, who isn't afraid of seeing, each night, a scowling spook in a butcher's apron with a display case full of, mostly, bagels and cream cheese above his head.

And they just don't hardly *make* that kind anymore.

VIOLATION

It is 2 a.m. and he waits. In the cool morning stillness of a side street, under the soft screen of trees, the rider waits quietly—at ease upon the wide leather seat of his cycle, gloved fingers resting idly on the bars, goggles up, eyes palely reflecting the leaf-filtered glow of the moon.

Helmeted. Uniformed. Waiting.

In the breathing dark, the cycle metal cools; the motor is silent, a power contained.

The faint stirrings of a still-sleeping city reach him at his vigil. But he is not concerned with these; he mentally dismisses them. He is concerned only with the broad river of smooth concrete facing him through the trees, and the great winking red eye suspended, icicle-like, above it.

He waits.

And tenses at a sound upon the river—an engine sound, mosquito-dim with distance, rising to a hum. A rushing sound under the stars.

The rider's hands contract like the claws of a bird. He rises slowly on the bucket seat, right foot poised near the starter. A coiled spring. Waiting.

Twin pencil-beams of light move towards him, towards the street on which he waits hidden. Closer.

The hum builds in volume; the lights are very close now, flaring chalk-white along the concrete boulevard.

The rider's goggles are down and he is ready to move out,

move on to the river. Another second, perhaps two ...

But no. The vehicle slows, makes a full stop. A service vehicle with two men inside, laughing, joking. The rider listens to them, mouth set, eyes hard. The vehicle begins to move once more. The sound is eaten by the night.

There is no violation.

Now ... the relaxing, the easing back. The ebb tide of tension receding. Gone. The rider quiet again under the moon.

Waiting.

The red eye winking at the empty boulevard.

'How much farther, Dave?' asks the girl.

'Ten miles, maybe. Once we hit Westwood, it's a quick run to my place. Relax. You're nervous.'

'We should have stayed on the mainway. Used the grid. I don't *like* these surface streets. A grid would have taken us in.'

The man smiles, looping an arm around her.

'There's nothing to be afraid of as long as you're careful,' he says. 'I used to drive surface streets all the time when I was a boy. Lots of people did.'

The girl swallows, touches her hair nervously. 'But they don't anymore. People use the grids. I didn't even know cars still *came* equipped for manual driving.'

'They don't. I had this set up by a mechanic I know. He does jobs like this for road buffs. It's still legal, driving your own car—it's just that most people have lost the habit.'

The girl peers out the window into the silent street, shakes her head. 'It's ... not natural. Look out there. Nobody! Not another car for miles. I feel as if we're trespassing.'

The man is annoyed. 'That's damn nonsense. I have friends who do this all the time. Just relax and enjoy it. And don't talk like an idiot.'

'I want out,' says the girl. 'I'll take a walkway back to the grid.'

'The hell you will,' flares the man. 'You're with *me* tonight. We're going to my place.'

She resists, strikes at his face; the man grapples to subdue her. He does not see the blinking light. The car passses under it, swiftly.

'Chrisdam!' snaps the man. 'I went through that light! You made me miss the stop. I've broken one of the surface laws!' He says this humbly.

'What does that mean?' the girl asks. 'What could happen?'

'Never mind. Nothing will happen. Never mind about what could happen.'

The girl peers out into the darkness. 'I want to leave this car.'

'Just shut up,' the man says, and keeps driving.

Something in the sound tells the rider that this one will not stop, that it will continue to move along the river of stone despite the blinking eye.

He smiles in the darkness, lips stretched back, silently. Poised there on the cycle, with the hum steady and rising on the river, he feels the power within him about to be released.

The car is almost upon the light, moving swiftly; there is no hint of slackened speed.

The rider watches intently. Man and a girl inside, struggling. Fighting with one another.

The car passes under the light.

Violation.

Now!

He spurs the cycle to metal life. The motor crackles, roars, explodes the black machine into motion, and the rider is away, rolling in muted thunder along the street. Around the corner, swaying on to the long, moon-painted river of the boulevard.

The rider feels the wind in his face, feels the throb and power-pulse of the metal thing he rides, feels the smooth concrete rushing backward under his wheels.

Ahead, the firefly glow of tail-lights.

And now his cycle cries out after them, a siren moan

through the still spaces of the city. A voice which rises and falls in spirals of sound. His cycle-eyes, mounted left and right, are blinking crimson, red as blood in their wake.

The car will stop. The man will see him, hear him. The eyes and the voice will reach the violator.

And he will stop.

'Bitch!' the man says. 'We've picked up a rider at that light.'

'*You* picked him up, I didn't,' says the girl. 'It's your problem.'

'But I've never been stopped on a surface street,' the man says, a desperate note in his voice. 'In all these years—never once!'

The girl glares at him. 'Dave, you make me sick! Look at you—shaking, sweating. You're a damn poor excuse for a man!'

He does not react to her words. He speaks in numbed monotone. 'I can talk my way out. I know I can. He'll listen to me. I have my rights as a citizen of the city.'

'He's catching up fast. You'd better pull over.'

His eyes harden as he brakes the car. 'I'll do the talking. All of it. You just keep quiet. I'll handle this.'

The rider sees that the car is slowing, braking, pulling to the kerb.

He cuts the siren voice, lets it die, glides the cycle in behind the car. Cuts the engine. Sits there for a long moment on the leather seat, pulling off his gloves. Slowly.

He sees the car door slide open. A man steps out, comes towards him. The rider swings a booted leg over the cycle and steps free, advancing to meet this law-breaker, fitting the gloves carefully into his black leather belt.

They face one another, the man smaller, paunchy, balding, face flushed. The rider's polite smile eases the man's tenseness.

'You in a hurry, sir?'

'Me? No, I'm not in a hurry. Not at all. It was just ...

I didn't *see* the light up there until . . . I was past it. The high trees and all. I swear to you. I didn't see it. I'd never knowingly break a surface law, Officer. You have my sworn word.'

Nervous. Shaken and nervous, this man. The rider can feel the man's guilt, a physical force. He extends a hand.

'May I see your operator's licence, please?'

The man fumbles in his coat. 'I have it right here. It's all in order, up to date and all.'

'Just let me see it, please.'

The man continues to talk.

'Been driving for years, Officer, and this is my first violation. Perfect record up to now. I'm a responsible citizen. I obey the laws. After all, I'm not a fool.'

The rider says nothing; he examines the man's licence, taps it thoughtfully against his wrist. The rider's goggles are opaque. The man cannot see his eyes as he studies the face of the violator.

'The woman in the car . . . is she your wife?'

'No. No, sir. She's . . . a friend. Just a friend.'

'Then why were you fighting? I saw the two of you fighting inside the car when it passed the light. That isn't friendly, is it?'

The man attempts to smile. 'Personal. We had a small personal disagreement. It's all over now, believe me.'

The rider walks to the car, leans to peer in at the woman. She is pale, as nervous as the man.

'You having trouble?' the rider asks.

She hesitates, shakes her head mutely. The rider leaves her and returns to the man, who is resting a hand against the cycle.

'Don't touch that,' says the rider coldly, and the man draws back his hand, mumbles an apology.

'I have no further use for this,' says the rider, handing back the man's licence. 'You are guilty of a surface-street violation.'

The man quakes; his hands tremble. 'But it was not *deliberate*. I know the law. You're empowered to make exceptions if a violation is not deliberate. The full penalty is not invoked in such cases. You are allowed to—'

The rider cuts into the flow of words. 'You forfeited your Citizen's Right of Exception when you allowed a primary emotion—anger, in this instance—to affect your control of a surface vehicle. Thus, my duty is clear and prescribed.'

The man's eyes widen in shock as the rider brings up a beltweapon. 'You can't possibly—'

'Under authorization of Citystate Overpopulation Statute 4452663, I am hereby executing ...'

The man begins to run.

'... sentence.'

He presses the trigger. Three long, probing blue jets of starshot flame leap from the weapon in the rider's hand.

The man is gone.

The woman is gone.

The car is gone.

The street is empty and silent. A charred smell of distant suns lingers in the morning air.

The rider stands by his cycle, unmoving for a long moment. Then he carefully holsters the weapon, pulls on his leather gloves. He mounts the cycle and it pulses to life under his foot.

With the sky in motion above him, he is again upon the moon-flowing boulevard, gliding back towards the blinking red eye.

The rider reaches his station on the small, tree-shadowed side street and thinks, *How stupid they are! To be subject to indecision, to quarrels and erratic behaviour—weak, all of them, Soft and weak.*

He smiles into the darkness.

The eye blinks over the river.

And now it is 4 a.m., now 6 and 8 and 10 and 1 p.m.... the hours turning like wheels, the days spinning away.

And he waits. Through nights without sleep, days without food—a flawless metal enforcer at his vigil, sure of himself and of his duty.

Waiting.

THE PARTY

Ashland frowned, trying to concentrate in the warm emptiness of the thickly carpeted lobby. Obviously, he had pressed the elevator button, because he was alone here and the elevator was blinking its way down to him, summoned from the upper floor. It arrived with an efficient hiss, the bronze doors clicked open, and he stepped in, thinking *blackout. I had a mental blackout.*

First the double vision. Now this. It was getting worse. He had blanked out completely. Just where the hell was he? Must be a party, he told himself. Sure. Someone he'd met, whose name was missing along with the rest of it, had invited him to a party. He had an apartment number in his head: 9E. That much he retained. A number—nothing else.

On the way up, in the soundless cage of the elevator, David Ashland reviewed the day. The usual morning routine: work, then lunch with his new secretary. A swinger—but she liked her booze; put away three martinis to his two. Back to the office. More work. A drink in the afternoon with a writer. ('Beefeater. No rocks. Very dry.') Dinner at the new Italian joint on West 48th with Linda. Lovely Linda. Expensive girl. Lovely as hell, but expensive. More drinks, then—nothing. Blackout.

The doc had warned him about the hard stuff, but what else can you do in New York? The pressures get to you, so you drink. Everybody drinks. And every night, somewhere in town, there's a party, with contacts (and girls) to be made ...

The elevator stopped, opened its doors. Ashland stepped out, uncertainly, into the hall. The softly lit passageway was long, empty, silent. No, not silent. Ashland heard the familiar voice of a party: the shifting hive hum of cocktail conversation, dim, high laughter, the sharp chatter of ice against glass, a background wash of modern jazz ... All quite familiar. And always the same.

He walked to 9E. Featureless apartment door. White. Brass button housing. Gold numbers. No clues here. Sighing, he thumbed the buzzer and waited nervously.

A smiling fat man with bad teeth opened the door. He was holding a half-filled drink in one hand. Ashland didn't know him.

'C'mon in, fella,' he said. 'Join the party.'

Ashland squinted into blue-swirled tobacco smoke, adjusting his eyes to the dim interior. The rising-falling sea tide of voices seemed to envelop him.

'Grab a drink, fella,' said the fat man. 'Looks like you need one!'

Ashland aimed for the bar in one corner of the crowded apartment. He *did* need a drink. Maybe a drink would clear his head, let him get this all straight. Thus far, he had not recognized any of the faces in the smoke-hazed room.

At the self-service bar a thin, turkey-necked woman wearing paste jewellery was intently mixing a black Russian. 'Got to be exceedingly careful with these,' she said to Ashland, eyes still on the mixture. 'Too much vodka craps them up.'

Ashland nodded. 'The host arrived?' *I'll know him, I'm sure.*

'Due later—or sooner. Sooner—or later. You know, I once spilled three black Russians on the same man over a thirty-day period. First on the man's sleeve, then on his back, then on his lap. Each time his suit was a sticky, gummy mess. My psychiatrist told me that I did it unconsciously, because of a neurotic hatred of this particular man. He looked like my father.'

'The psychiatrist?'

'No, the man I spilled the black Russians on.' She held up the tall drink, sipped at it. 'Ahhh . . . still too weak.'

Ashland probed the room for a face he knew, but these people were all strangers.

He turned to find the turkey-necked woman staring at him. 'Nice apartment,' he said mechanically.

'Stinks. I detest pseudo-Chinese decor in Manhattan

brownstones.' She moved off, not looking back at Ashland.

He mixed himself a straight Scotch, running his gaze around the apartment. The place *was* pretty wild—ivory tables with serpent legs; tall, figured screens with chain-mail warriors cavorting across them; heavy brocade drapes in stitched silver; lamps with jewel-eyed dragons looped at the base. And, at the far end of the room, an immense bronze gong suspended between a pair of demon-faced swordsmen. Ashland studied the gong. A thing to wake the dead, he thought. Great for hangovers in the morning.

'Just get here?' a girl asked him. She was red-haired, full-breasted, in her late twenties. Attractive. Damned attractive. Ashland smiled warmly at her.

'That's right,' he said. 'I just arrived.' He tasted the Scotch; it was flat, watery. 'Whose place is this?'

The girl peered at him above her cocktail glass. 'Don't you know who invited you?'

Ashland was embarrassed. 'Frankly, no. That's why I—'

'My name's Viv. For Vivian. I drink. What do you do? Besides drink?'

'I produce. I'm in television.'

'Well, *I'm* in a dancing mood. Shall we?'

'Nobody's dancing,' protested Ashland. 'We'd look—foolish.'

The jazz suddenly seemed louder. Overhead speakers were sending out a thudding drum solo behind muted strings. The girl's body rippled to the sounds.

'Never be afraid to do anything foolish,' she told him. 'That's the secret of survival.' Her fingers beckoned him. 'C'mon . . .'

'No, really—not right now. Maybe later.'

'Then I'll dance alone.'

She spun into the crowd, her long red dress whirling. The other partygoers ignored her. Ashland emptied the watery Scotch and fixed himself another. He loosened his tie, popping the collar button. *Damn!*

'I train worms.'

Ashland turned to a florid-faced little man with bulging,

feverish eyes. 'I heard you say you were in TV,' the little man said. 'Ever use any trained worms on your show?'

'No . . . no, we don't.'

'I breed 'em, train 'em. I teach a worm to run a maze. Then I grind him up and feed him to a dumb, untrained worm. Know what happens? The dumb worm can run the maze! But only for twenty-four hours. Then he forgets—unless I keep him on a trained-worm diet. I defy you to tell me that isn't fascinating!'

'It is, indeed.' Ashland nodded and moved away from the bar. The feverish little man smiled after him, toasting his departure with a raised glass. Ashland found himself sweating.

Who was his host? Who had invited him? He knew most of the Village crowd, but had spotted none of them here . . .

A dark, doll-like girl asked him for a light. He fumbled out some matches.

'Thanks,' she said, exhaling blue smoke into blue smoke. 'Saw that worm guy talking to you. What a lousy bore *he* is! My ex-husband had a pet snake named Baby and he fed it worms. That's all they're good for, unless you fish. Do you fish?'

'I've done some fishing up in Canada.'

'My ex-husband hated all sports. Except the indoor variety.' She giggled. 'Did you hear the one about the indoor hen and the outdoor rooster?'

'Look, Miss—'

'Talia. But you can call me Jenny. Get it?' she doubled over, laughing hysterically, then swayed, dropping her cigarette. 'Ooops! I'm sick. I better go lie down. My tum-tum feels awful.'

She staggered from the party as Ashland crushed out her smouldering cigarette with the heel of his shoe. *Stupid bitch!*

A sharp handclap startled him. In the middle of the room, a tall man in a green satin dinner jacket was demanding his attention. He clapped again. 'You,' he shouted to Ashland. 'Come here.'

Ashland walked forward. The tall man asked him to remove his wrist watch. 'I'll read your past from it,' the man said. 'I'm psychic. I'll tell you about yourself.'

Reluctantly, Ashland removed his watch, handed it over. He didn't find any of this amusing. The party was annoying him, irritating him.

'I thank you most kindly, sir!' said the tall man, with elaborate stage courtesy. He placed the gold watch against his forehead and closed his eyes, breathing deeply. The crowd noise did not slacken; no one seemed to be paying any attention to the psychic.

'Ah. Your name is David. David Ashland. You are successful, a man of big business ... a producer ... and a bachelor. You are twenty-eight ... very young for a successful producer. One has to be something of a bastard to climb that fast. What about that, Mr. Ashland, *are* you something of a bastard?'

Ashland flushed angrily.

'You like women,' continued the tall man. 'A lot. And you like to drink. A lot. Your doctor told you—'

'I don't have to listen to this,' Ashland said tightly, reaching for his watch. The man in green satin handed it over, grinned amiably, and melted back into the shifting crowd.

I ought to get the hell out of here, Ashland told himself. Yet curiosity held him. When the host arrived, Ashland would piece this evening together; he'd know why he was there, at this particular party. He moved to a couch near the closed patio doors and sat down. He'd wait.

A soft-faced man sat down next to him. The man looked pained. 'I shouldn't smoke these,' he said, holding up a long cigar. 'Do you smoke cigars?'

'No.'

'I'm a salesman. Dover Insurance. Like the White Cliffs of, ya know. I've studied the problems involved in smoking. Can't quit, though. When I do, the nerves shrivel up, stomach goes sour. I worry a lot—but we all worry, don't we? I mean, my mother used to worry about the earth slowing down. She read somewhere that between 1680 and

1690 the earth lost twenty-seven hundredths of a second. She said that meant something.'

Ashland sighed inwardly. What is it about cocktail parties that causes people you've never met to instantly unleash their troubles?

'You meet a lotta fruitcakes in my dodge,' said the pained-looking insurance salesman. 'I sold a policy once to a guy who lived in the woodwork. Had a ratty little walk-up in the Bronx with a foldaway bed. Kind you push into the wall. He'd *stay* there—I mean, inside the wall—most of the time. His roommate would invite some friends in and if they made too much noise the guy inside the wall would pop out with his Thompson. BAM! The bed would come down and there he was with a Thompson submachine gun aimed at everybody. Real fruitcake.'

'I knew a fellow who was *twice* that crazy.'

Ashland looked up into a long, cadaverous face. The nose had been broken and improperly reset; it canted noticeably to the left. He folded his long, sharp-boned frame on to the couch next to Ashland. 'The fellow believed in falling grandmothers,' he declared. 'Lived in upper Michigan. "Watch out for falling grandmothers," he used to warn me. "They come down pretty heavy in this area. Most of 'em carry umbrellas and big packages and they come flapping down out of the sky by the thousands!" This Michigan fellow swore he saw one hit a postman. "An awful thing to watch," he told me. "Knocked the poor soul flat. Crushed his skull like an egg." I recall he shuddered just telling me about it.'

'Fruitcake,' said the salesman. 'Like the guy I once knew who wrote on all his walls and ceilings. A creative writer, he called himself. Said he couldn't write on paper, had to use a wall. Paper was too flimsy for him. He'd scrawl these long novels of his, a chapter in every room, with a big black crayon. Words all over the place. He'd fill up the house, then rent another one for his next book. I never read any of his houses, so I don't know if he was any good.'

'Excuse me, gentlemen,' said Ashland. 'I need a fresh drink.'

He hurriedly mixed another Scotch at the bar. Around him, the party rolled on inexorably, without any visible core. What time was it, anyway? His watch had stopped.

'Do you happen to know what time it is?' he asked a long-haired Oriental girl who was standing near the bar.

'I've no idea,' she said. 'None at all.' The girl fixed him with her eyes. 'I've been watching you, and you seem horribly *alone*. Aren't you?'

'Aren't I what?'

'Horribly alone?'

'I'm not with anyone, if that's what you mean.'

The girl withdrew a jewelled holder from her bag and fitted a cigarette in place. Ashland lit it for her.

'I haven't been really alone since I was in Milwaukee,' she told him. 'I was about—God!—fifteen or something, and this creep wanted me to move in with him. My parents were both dead by then, so I was all alone.'

'What did you do?'

'Moved in with the creep. What else? I couldn't make the being-alone scene. Later on, I killed him.'

'You *what?*'

'Cut his throat.' She smiled delicately. 'In self-defence, of course. He got mean on the bottle one Friday night and tried to knife me. I had witnesses.'

Ashland took a long draw on his Scotch. A scowling fellow in shirt-sleeves grabbed the girl's elbow and steered her roughly away.

'I used to know a girl who looked like that,' said a voice to Ashland's right. The speaker was curly-haired, clean-featured, in his late thirties. 'Greek belly dancer with a Jersey accent. Dark, like her, and kind of mysterious. She used to quote that line of Hemingway's to Scott Fitzgerald—you know the one.'

'Afraid not.'

'One that goes, "We're all bitched from the start." Bitter. A bitter line.'

He put out his hand. Ashland shook it.

'I'm Travers. I used to save America's ass every week on CBS.'

'Beg pardon?'

'Terry Travers. The old *Triple Trouble for Terry* series on channel nine. Back in the late fifties. Had to step on a lotta toes to get that series.'

'I think I recall the show. It was—'

'Dung. That's what it was. Cow dung. Horse dung. The *worst*. Terry Travers is not my real name, natch. Real one's Abe Hockstatter. Can you imagine a guy named Abe Hockstatter saving America's ass every week on CBS?'

'You've got me there.'

Hockstatter pulled a brown wallet from his coat, flipped it open. 'There I am with one of my other rugs on,' he said, jabbing at a photo. 'Been stone bald since high school. Baldies don't make it in showbiz, so I have my rugs. Go ahead, tug at me.'

Ashland blinked. The man inclined his head. '*Pull* at it. Go on—as a favour to me!'

Ashland tugged at the fringe of Abe Hockstatter's curly hairpiece.

'Tight, eh? Really *snug*. Stays on the old dome.'

'Indeed it does.'

'They cost a fortune. I've got a wind-blown one for outdoor scenes. A stiff wind'll lift a cheap rug right off your scalp. Then I got a crew cut and a Western job with long sideburns. All kinds. Ten, twelve ... all first-class.'

'I'm certain I've seen you,' said Ashland. 'I just don't—'

' 'S awright. Believe me. Lotta people don't know me since I quit the *Terry* thing. I booze like crazy now. You an' me, we're among the nation's six million alcoholics.'

Ashland glared at the actor. 'Where do you get off linking me with—'

'Cool it, cool it. So I spoke a little out of turn. Don't be so touchy, chum.'

'To hell with you!' snapped Ashland.

The bald man with curly hair shrugged and drifted into the crowd.

Ashland took another long pull at his Scotch. All these neurotic conversations ... He felt exhausted, wrung dry, and the Scotch was lousy. No kick to it. The skin along the back of his neck felt tight, hot. A headache was coming on; he could always tell.

A slim-figured, frosted blonde in black sequins sidled up to him. She exuded an aura of matrimonial wars fought and lost. Her orange lipstick was smeared, her cheeks alcohol-flushed behind flaking pancake make-up. 'I have a theory about sleep,' she said. 'Would you like to hear it?'

Ashland did not reply.

'My theory is that the world goes insane every night. When we sleep, our subconscious takes charge and we become victims to whatever it conjures up. Our conscious, reasoning mind is totally blanked out. We lie there, helpless, while our subconscious flings us about. We fall off high buildings, or have to fight a giant ape, or we get buried in quicksand ... We have absolutely no control. The mind whirls madly in the skull. Isn't that an unsettling thing to consider?'

'Listen,' said Ashland. 'Where's the host?'

'He'll get here.'

Ashland put down his glass and turned away from her. A mounting wave of depression swept him towards the door. The room seemed to be solid with bodies, all talking, drinking, gesturing in the milk-thick smoke haze.

'Potatoes have eyes,' said a voice to his left. 'I really *believe* that.' The remark was punctuated by an ugly, frog-croaking laugh.

'Today is tomorrow's yesterday,' someone else said.

A hot swarm of sound:

'You can't get prints off human skin.'

'In China, the labourers make sixty-five dollars a year. How the hell can you live on sixty-five dollars a year?'

'So he took out this Luger and blew her head off.'

'I knew a policewoman who loved to scrub down whores.'

'Did you ever try to live with eight kids, two dogs, a three-legged cat and twelve goldfish?'

'Like I told him, those X-rays destroyed his white cells.'

'They found her in the tub. Strangled with a coat hanger.'

'What I had, exactly, was a grade-two epidermoid carcinoma at the base of a seborrheac keratosis.'

Ashland experienced a sudden, raw compulsion: Somehow he had to stop these voices!

The Chinese gong flared gold at the corner of his eye. He pushed his way over to it, shouldering the partygoers aside. He would strike it—and the booming noise would stun the crowd; they'd have to stop their incessant, maddening chatter.

Ashland drew back his right fist, then drove it into the circle of bronze. He felt the impact, and the gong shuddered under his blow.

But there was no sound from it!

The conversation went on.

Ashland smashed his way back across the apartment.

'You can't stop the party,' said the affable fat man at the door.

'I'm leaving!'

'So go ahead,' grinned the fat man. 'Leave.'

Ashland clawed open the door and plunged into the hall, stumbling, almost falling. He reached the elevator, jabbed at the DOWN button.

Waiting, he found it impossible to swallow; his throat was dry. He could feel his heart hammering against the walls of his chest. His head ached.

The elevator arrived, opened. He stepped inside. The doors closed smoothly and the cage began its slow, automatic descent.

Abruptly, it stopped.

The doors parted to admit a solemn-looking man in a dark blue suit.

Ashland gasped 'Freddie!'

The solemn face broke into a wide smile. 'Dave! It's great to see you! Been—a long time.'

'But—you can't be Fred Baker!'

'Why? Have I changed so much?'

'No, no, you look—exactly the same. But that car crash in Albany. I thought you were ...' Ashland hesitated, left the word unspoken. He was pale, frightened. Very frightened. 'Look, I'm—I'm late. Got somebody waiting for me at my place. Have to rush ...' He reached forward to push the LOBBY button.

There was none.

The lowest button read FLOOR 2.

'We use this elevator to get from one party to another,' Freddie Baker said quietly, as the cage surged into motion. 'That's all it's good for. You get so you need a change. They're all alike, though—the parties. But you learn to adjust, in time. We all have.'

Ashland stared at his departed friend. The elevator stopped.

'Step out,' said Freddie. 'I'll introduce you around. You'll catch on, get used to things. No sex here. And the booze is watered. Can't get stoned. That's the dirty end of the stick.'

Baker took Ashland's arm, propelled him gently forward.

Around him, pressing in, David Ashland could hear familiar sounds: nervous laughter, ice against glass, muted jazz—and the ceaseless hum of cocktail voices.

Freddie thumbed a buzzer. A door opened.

The smiling fat man said, 'C'mon in, fellas. Join the party.'

PAPA'S PLANET

Of the late Harrington Hunter Hollister, it must be said that he was very rich, that he had sired a beautiful man-chasing redhead, and that he was a Hemingway fanatic. When he died in 2068, I ended up with his money, his newly divorced daughter, and his Hemingway collection.

'As my latest and absolutely *last* husband, I want you to

have everything,' Cecile Hollister told me, wrinkling her attractively freckled nose. 'Daddy adored you.'

'I adored daddy,' I said, trying for sincerity.

She handed me a rolled parchment.

'What's this?' I asked.

'A deed to Papa's Planet. I've never been there, but daddy told me all about it. That's where we're spending our honeymoon.'

'We are?'

'You want to see your property, don't you?'

'I guess so.'

'We'll leave tomorrow.'

Cecile had a way with men.

We left tomorrow.

Five million miles out from Mars, we turned sharp left and there it was: Papa's Planet—a big grey ball of matter floating below us.

'What the devil's *down* there?' I asked.

'You'll find out. Strap in. Here we go.'

We made a fine soft-point landing (Cecile could handle a Spacer like a pro) and, when the rocket smoke cleared, I saw a big, wide-chested fellow in khaki hunting clothes approaching us. He was bearded, grizzled, with suspicious eyes. And he carried an elephant gun.

'You critics?' he demanded.

'Hardly,' said Cecile. 'I'm the daughter of Harrington Hollister and this is my new husband Philip.'

'OK, then,' said the bearded man, pivoting. 'I'm hunting critics. See any, give me a yell.'

'Will do,' said Cecile. And to me: 'C'mon, Pamplona should be right on the other side of the mountain. We can catch the running of the bulls.'

'Who was the aggressive bearded guy?'

'Papa, of course. It's his planet.'

Running along next to me, just in front of the bulls, a strong-looking guy thumped my shoulder and yelled, 'This is swell, isn't it!'

'Yeah, swell!' I yelled back, sprinting to catch Cecile. 'Who's the guy back there, yelling?'

'Papa,' she told me. 'Only he's a lot younger, naturally. This is 1923. Hey, let's cut through this side street. I want to see Paris.'

Paris was right next to Pamplona, and Cecile looked radiant walking down the Rue de la Paix. 'I'd love to meet Gertrude Stein,' she said. 'Maybe we can have lunch with her.'

A big guy with a moustache pounded past us in a half crouch, feinting at the air with left and right jabs. He was dark-haired, tough-looking. 'Hi, daughter,' he said to Cecile.

'Hi, Ernie,' she called back.

He padded away.

'Wait a damn minute,' I said. 'Who was *that*?'

She sighed. 'Papa, naturally. Only nobody calls him Papa in Paris. Too early. Wrong period.'

'Just how many Papas *are* there?'

Cecile stopped and wrinkled her nose. 'Well, let's see ... at least twenty that I know of, and I'm no expert. That was daddy's department.'

'And they're *all* here?'

'Sure.' She pointed. 'Just beyond Paris, across the Seine, is Oak Park, Illinois—which is next to Walloon Lake, Michigan. That's two Papas right there, one for each place. Both are *boy* Papas, of course. One goes to Oak Park High and the other goes trout fishing on the lake.'

I nodded. 'We've got one here—and another in Pamplona. And there's the one we met near the rocket.'

'That was the African one,' she said. 'Then there's the one in New York with the hairy chest who keeps standing Max Eastman on his head in the corner of Scribner's. And the Papa in the hills of Spain covering the civil war and the one skiing in Switzerland with Hadley and the one on the Gulf Stream in the *Pilar*—daddy dug out a lovely Gulf Stream and I can't wait to see it—and there's the one getting shot in the kneecap somewhere in Italy.'

'Fossalta di Piave,' I supplied.

'That's the place,' she said, pushing back a strand of delicious red hair. 'And there's the Papa in Key West and the one in Venice and the one boxing in the gym in Kansas City. How many is that?'

'I've lost count,' I said.

'Anyway, there are *lots* more,' said Cecile. 'Daddy had his whole factory in Des Moines working overtime for six months, including weekends, just to supply all the Papas.'

'Probably one camped out by the Big Two-Hearted River?

'Sure. And another in Toronto, working for the *Star*.'

I raised an eyebrow. 'Must have cost your dad plenty.'

'It was a tax write-off,' she said. 'Nonprofit. Besides, he had this big empty planet just going to *waste* up here.'

'But—building Paris in the twenties and the streets of Pamplona and the bull rings of Spain and all of Africa—'

'He didn't build *all* of Africa,' Cecile corrected me. 'Just the important part around Kilimanjaro, where we landed.'

'Don't the Papas get mixed up, bump into each other?'

'Never. Each Papa has his assigned place and that's where he stays, doing what he was built for. The Pamplona Papa just keeps running with the bulls, and the African Papa keeps hunting critics.'

'Your father sure didn't stint.'

'When daddy did a thing, he did it *right*,' she agreed. 'Now, let's go have lunch with Miss Stein and then visit Venice. Daddy said they did a marvellous job with St. Mark's Square.'

Papa was drinking alone at a table near the Grand Canal when our gondola passed by, and he waved us over.

'You smell good, daughter,' Papa told Cecile. 'You smell the way good leather you find in the little nonsense shops in Madrid when you know enough not to get suckered into the big shops that charge too much smells.'

'Thanks, Papa,' said Cecile, giving him a bright smile.

'I always enjoy the Gritti here in Venice,' said Papa, 'and ordering a strong lobster who had much heart and who died properly, and having him served to you by a waiter you can trust with a good bottle of Capri near you so you can see the little green ice bubbles form on the cold glass.'

He poured us wine. We all saluted one another and drank. The sun went down and the wine made me sleepy.

When I awoke, Cecile was gone.

I said good-bye to Papa and went out to look for her.

She wasn't at Key West, or on the Gulf, or anywhere in Spain, or in Billings, Montana (where Papa was recovering from his auto accident). I finally found her in Paris. On the Left Bank.

'I've fallen in love,' she declared. 'You can go on back to Earth and forget me.'

I shrugged. Cecile was hardly steadfast; as her fourth husband, I realized that. 'Who is he?'

'I call him Ougly-poo. That's my special love name for him. He just adores it.'

'He isn't human, is he?'

'Of course not!' She looked annoyed. 'We're the only *people* on Papa's Planet. But what difference does that make?'

'No difference, I guess.'

'He's divine.' She smiled dreamily, wrinkling her freckles. 'Kind of a classic profile, soft, sensitive lips, exciting eyes ... He gave me this autographed picture. See?'

I looked at it. 'You're sure?'

'I'm sure,' she said.

'OK, then,' I said. ''Bye, Cecile.'

''Bye, Philip.' She threw me a kiss.

I walked back to the rocket through a sad, softly falling Hemingway rain. I didn't blame Cecile. The fellow was handsome, witty, brilliant, famous. All the things I wasn't. Girls weren't inspired to call me Ougly-poo.

But then, I wasn't F. Scott Fitzgerald.

DARK WINNER

NOTE: The following is an edited transcript of a taped conversation between Mrs. Franklin Evans, resident of Woodland Hills, California, and Lt. Harry W. Lyle of the Kansas City Police Department.

Transcript is dated July 12, 1975. K.C. Missouri

LYLE: ... and if you want us to help you we'll have to know everything. When did you arrive here, Mrs. Evans?

MRS. EVANS: We just got in this morning. A stopover on our trip from New York back to California. We were at the airport when Frank suddenly got this idea about his past.

LYLE: What idea?

MRS. E: About visiting his old neighbourhood ... the school he went to ... the house where he grew up ... He hadn't been back here in twenty-five years.

LYLE: So you and your husband planned this ... nostalgic tour?

MRS. E: Not *planned*. It was very abrupt ... Frank seemed ... suddenly ... *possessed* by the idea.

LYLE: So what happened?

MRS. E: We took a cab out to Flora Avenue ... to 31st ... and we visited his old grade school. St. Vincent's Academy. The neighbourhood is ... well, I guess you know it's a slum area now ... and the school is closed down, locked. But Frank found an open window ... climbed inside ...

LYLE: While you waited?

MRS. E: Yes—in the cab. When Frank came out he was all upset ... Said that he ... Well, this sounds ...

LYLE: Go on, please.

MRS. E: He said he felt ... very *close* to his childhood while he was in there. He was ashen-faced ... his hands were trembling.

LYLE: What did you do then?

MRS. E: We had the cab take us up 31st to the Isis Theatre. The movie house at 31st and Troost where Frank used to attend those Saturday horror shows they had for kids. Each week a new one ... Frankenstein ... Dracula ... you know the kind I mean.

LYLE: I know.

MRS. E: It's a porno place now ... but Frank bought a ticket anyway ... went inside alone. Said he wanted to go into the balcony, find his old seat ... see if things had changed ...

LYLE: And?

MRS. E: He came out looking very shaken ... saying it had happened again.

LYLE: *What* had happened again?

MRS. E: The feeling about being close to his past ... to his childhood ... As if he could—

LYLE: Could what, Mrs. Evans?

MRS. E: ... step over the line dividing past and present ... step back into childhood. That's the feeling he said he had.

LYLE: Where did you go from the Isis?

MRS. E: Frank paid off the cab ... said he wanted to walk to his old block ... the one he grew up on ... 33rd and Forest. So we walked down Troost to 33rd ... past strip joints and hamburger stands ... I was nervous ... we didn't ... belong here ... Anyway, we got to 33rd and walked down the hill from Troost to Forest ... and on the way Frank told me how much he'd hated being small, being a child ... that he could hardly wait to grow up ... that to him childhood was a nightmare ...

LYLE: Then why all the nostalgia?

MRS. E: It wasn't that ... it was an *exorcism* ... Frank said he'd been haunted by his childhood all the years we'd lived in California ... This was an attempt to get rid of it ... by facing it ... seeing that it was really gone ... that it no longer had any reality ...

LYLE: What happened on Forest?

MRS. E: We walked down the street to his old address ... which was just past the middle of the block ... 3337 it was ... a small, sagging wooden house ... in terrible condition ... but then, *all* the houses were ... their screens full of holes ... windows broken, trash in the yards ... Frank stood in front of his house staring at it for a long time ... and then he began repeating something ... over and over.

LYLE: And what was that?

MRS. E: He said it ... like a litany ... over and over ... 'I hate you! ... I hate you! ... I hate you!'

LYLE: You mean, he was saying that to *you*?

MRS. E: Oh, no. Not to *me* ... I asked him what he meant ... and ... he said he hated the child he once was, the child who had lived in that house.

LYLE: I see. Go on, Mrs Evans.

MRS. E: Then he said he was going inside ... that he *had* to go inside the house ... but that he was afraid.

LYLE: Of what?

MRS. E: He didn't say of what. He just told me to wait out there on the walk. Then he went up on to the small wooden porch ... knocked on the door. No one answered. Then Frank tried the knob ... The door was unlocked ...

LYLE: House was deserted?

MRS. E: That's right. I guess no one had lived there for a long while ... All the windows were boarded up ... and the driveway was filled with weeds ... I started to move towards the porch, but Frank waved me back. Then he kicked the door all the way open with his foot, took a half-step inside, turned ... and looked back at me ... There was ... a terrible fear in his eyes. I got a cold, chilled feeling all through my body—and I started towards him again ... but he suddenly turned his back and went inside ... the door closed.

LYLE: What then?

MRS. E: Then I waited. For fifteen ... twenty minutes ... a half hour ... Frank didn't come out. So I went up to the porch and opened the door ... called to him ...

LYLE: Any answer?

MRS. E: No. The house was like ... a hollow cave ... there were echoes ... but no answer ... I went inside ... walked all through the place ... into every room ... but he wasn't there ... Frank was gone.

LYLE: Out the back, maybe.

MRS. E: No. The back door was nailed shut. Rusted. It hadn't been opened for years.

LYLE: A window then.

MRS. E: They were all boarded over. With thick dust on the sills.

LYLE: Did you check the basement?

MRS. E: Yes, I checked the basement door leading down. It was locked, and the dust hadn't been disturbed around it.

LYLE: Then ... just where the hell did he *go*?

MRS. E: I don't *know*, Lieutenant! ... That's why I called you ... why I came here ... You've got to find Frank!

END FIRST TRANSCRIPT

NOTE: Lt. Lyle did not find Franklin Evans. The case was turned over to Missing Persons—and, a week later, Mrs. Evans returned to her home in California. The first night back she had a dream, a nightmare. It disturbed her severely. She could not eat, could not sleep properly; her nerves were shattered. Mrs. Evans then sought psychiatric help. What follows is an excerpt from a taped session with Dr. Lawrence Redding, a licensed psychiatrist with offices in Beverly Hills, California.

Transcript is dated August 3, 1975. Beverly Hills

REDDING: And where were you ...? In the dream, I mean.

MRS. E: My bedroom. In bed, at home. It was as if I'd just been awakened ... I looked around me—and everything was normal ... the room exactly as it always is ... Except for *him* ... the boy standing next to me.

REDDING: Did you recognize this boy?

MRS. E: No.

REDDING: Describe him to me.

MRS. E: He was ... nine or ten ... a *horrible* child ... with a cold hate in his face, in his eyes ... He had on a red sweater with holes in each elbow. And knickers ... the kind that boys used to wear ... and he had on black tennis shoes ...

REDDING: Did he speak to you?

MRS. E: Not at first. He just ... smiled at me ... and that smile was so ... so evil! ... And then he said ... that he wanted me to know he'd won at last ...

REDDING: Won what?

MRS. E: That's what I asked him ... calmly, in the dream ... I asked him what he'd won. And he said ... oh, My God ... he said ...

REDDING: Go on, Mrs. Evans.

MRS. E: ... that he'd won Frank! ... that my husband would *never* be coming back ... that he, the boy, had him now ... forever! ... I screamed—and woke up. And, instantly, I remembered something.

REDDING: What did you remember?

MRS. E: Before she died ... Frank's mother ... sent us an album she'd saved ... of his childhood ... photos ... old report cards ... He never wanted to look at it, stuck the album away in a closet ... After the dream, I got it out, looked through it until I found ...

REDDING: Yes ...?

MRS. E: A photo I'd remembered. Of Frank ... at the age of ten ... standing in the front yard on Forest ... He was smiling ... that same, awful smile ... and ... he wore a sweater with holes in each elbow ... and knickers ... black tennis shoes. It was ... the *same* boy exactly—the younger self Frank had always hated ... I *know* what happened in that house now.

REDDING: Then tell me.

MRS. E: The boy was ... waiting there ... inside that awful, rotting dead house ... waiting for Frank to come back ... all those years ... waiting there to claim him—because ... *he* hated the man that Frank had become as much as Frank hated the child he'd once been ... and the boy was *right*.

REDDING: Right about what, Mrs. Evans?

MRS. E: About winning ... He took all those years, but ... He won ... and ... Frank lost.

END TRANSCRIPT

OPERATION GORF

There's a special office at the Pentagon called the Office of Stateside Emergencies. Dave Merkle is in charge, a thin, night-eyed man, haunted by a perpetual sense of failure. He was depressed on the morning of June 3, 1983 because there had not been a decent stateside emergency since early May. There had been three superb overseas emergencies, but they were handled by another office down the hall and didn't count.

The morning of June 3 was when Dave Merkle's right-hand man, troubleshooter Eldon Sash, came in smiling. 'We got one,' he said.

Merkle raised his head from the desk to peer at Sash, who was fat and jolly. 'Emergency?'

'You bet,' said Sash in a piping voice. Fat men often have them.

'Stateside?'

'Right in upper New York.'

Merkle looked dubious. He rose slowly from his chair. 'I just hope this is a spot-on, one hundred percent goddamn emergency.'

'It's a frog.'

'A frog in upper New York State is no emergency.' He sat down again.

'This one is,' Sash persisted. 'It's big.'

'How big?'

'I'd say about the size of your average four-unit apartment house.'

'That's big all right,' said Dave Merkle, thoughtfully tapping his chin. He began to look pleased.

'And it eats people. It already ate a guy in a sports car.'

'What make?'

Sash carefully removed a small green notebook from his coat, checked a page. 'Corvette.'

Merkle smacked his palms together. 'I *like* it, Eldon, I like it!' He strapped on a custom-grip .38 service revolver which was officially licensed and registered. 'Where's the frog now?'

'After it ate the Corvette, it hopped off towards Sleepy Hollow.'

'Fine. I'll have a chopper pick us up on the roof and we'll hustle right out there.' He gripped Sash at the elbow.

'Sir?'

'We need a project name for this thing. Any suggestions?'

'How about Gorf? Project Gorf.'

'I don't get it.' Merkle looked disturbed.

'That's frog spelled backwards,' Sash told him.

'Gorf! Gorf! Gorf! It's a buy, Eldon! I'll have Miss Hennessey make up a folder.'

'Meet you on the roof,' piped Sash.

On the way to Sleepy Hollow in the Washington copter Merkle wanted to know how the frog got so big.

'It gobbled up some experimental growth pellets,' Sash explained.

'Ours? Or *theirs*?' Merkle frowned.

'Neither,' Sash replied. 'So far as I know, our government is not working on any such pellet. Nor is Red China. These particular growth pellets come from the lab of a cranky old eccentric. As I get it, he was developing the pellets for use on ducks. Planned to raise giant ducks for personal profit, claiming that future generations could live on expanded duckmeat. The pellets were designed solely for ducks, but the frog got 'em.'

'How?'

'A crate of duck pellets fell out of his pickup truck as he was crossing a bog, and he didn't miss 'em until he got home. By then, it was too late. This frog ate the whole crateful.'

'I see,' said Merkle, tapping his chin. 'Any more pellets left?'

'Not according to the old eccentric's pretty niece, a girl named Pinning. She told me her uncle just had this one crate. But he could make more.'

'Nix on that.' Merkle swept his hand out in a negative gesture. 'Spiders could get 'em. Next thing, we have a giant three-storey spider. Or a train-sized snake. No good.'

'I told her to tell him to hold up on 'em until we could make an official decision.'

'I'll get Miss Hennessey to issue a freeze form,' declared Merkle. 'Make it illegal for the old bastard to produce any more of the things.'

The copter pilot announced that they were in the direct vicinity of Sleepy Hollow.

'I don't see any mammoth frog down there,' Merkle snapped, shading his eyes. 'What about that, Eldon?'

'It could be behind a small mountain digesting the sports car.'

'Okay, then. We'll head for the old eccentric. He might have a lead on where the damned thing is.'

The copter whipsawed west.

Linda Pinning led Merkle and Sash towards the laboratory of her uncle. She was a starkly-beautiful girl of nineteen, with luminous skin and long dancer's legs. She wore a black leotard. 'I'm a victim of schizoid conflict,' she confided as they moved down a long hallway. 'My Uncle Downey thinks I possess remarkable talent, but I personally *loathe* toe-dancing.'

'What *do* you prefer?' asked Merkle.

'Swamp life!' She sucked in a breath excitedly, and her breasts trembled. 'That's why I live here with Uncle Downey. I've become an expert on swamp life. Garter snakes. Water bugs. And, of course, ducks.'

'Of course,' said Merkle.

They entered the lab. 'My uncle is upstairs, but I thought you'd want to get a look in here first. You can see the success he's already had with pumpkins.'

The lab was full of giant pumpkins.

'Must be ten times their natural size,' commented Sash, absently patting his pumpkin stomach.

'Easily,' agreed Merkle.

Linda explained why her uncle had switched to ducks. 'He felt that pumpkins were too limited.'

Sash grinned. 'Sure can't roast a pumpkin!'

'We just want to know about the frog,' Merkle said, scowling. 'I suggest you fetch your uncle.'

Linda complied, and moments later a dark hairy old man wearing a frayed black ankle-length raincoat tottered into the lab. His eyes bugged fiercely at them from incredibly thick-lensed glasses.

'Make it quick,' he said. 'Make it quick.'

Merkle asked about the frog.

'None of my affair,' grumped the old man. 'Damn frog's none of my affair!'

'Ah, but it *is*,' Merkle corrected him. 'Your growth pellets caused it to expand into a public menace. It has already eaten a Corvette driver. We're here on emergency status.'

'Don't care. Don't care a pig's snout for your status!' He produced a rolled umbrella from inside the coat and waved it threateningly.

'My uncle's a Nauruan,' Linda told them, by way of apology. 'They get cranky in their old age.'

'I never heard of the place,' said Merkle.

'Naura is an island nation of six thousand,' Sash flatly

intoned, 'covering an area of eight square miles, located south of the equator and northeast of the Solomon Islands. You can look it up in the Cowles *Encyclopedia of Nations*.'

The awkward impasse was broken by a loud trumpeting sound from the woods beyond the house.

'I think that's him, chief,' said Sash.

'That is certainly the amplified croak of a *Rana catesbeiana*, or common bullfrog,' Linda agreed.

Merkle whipped out his custom-grip revolver. 'Let's pepper him!'

'Won't do any good,' declared the cranky old man. 'Bullets will just bounce off. Couldn't kill him with a cannon.'

'What's he talking about?' demanded Merkle.

'Unfortunately, one of the present flaws in my Uncle Downey's growth-pellet research is the peculiar effect produced on the outer layers of any living creature. What you'll encounter is an armour-like exterior, impervious to bullets.'

'That's crazy,' sneered Eldon Sash. 'How could people eat impervious ducks?'

'Exactly the problem my uncle is attempting to overcome,' said Linda.

Merkle began to look desperate. 'If an armoured frog starts hopping towards New York, my fat's in the fire! What kind of ground can it cover?'

The girl clucked her tongue. 'At its present size, it can traverse up to fifty miles at a hop.'

The old man stomped his foot. 'All right, all right. I'll deal with it. I can deal with it. I've dealt with worse.'

And he tottered briskly from the lab.

They crashed through the afternoon woods in the wake of the old man, attempting to keep up with his green battery car.

'How can he drive that thing in this kind of country?' asked Sash, out of breath and staggering.

'He's converted to off-road-vehicle components,' panted the running girl. 'Uncle Downey can go anywhere now.'

'Hardly keep him in sight,' gasped Dave Merkle, trotting

beside Linda.

They entered a swampy area where huge, gaseous bubbles churned at ground surface. The green battery car, with its notched doughnut tyres, was parked at the edge of the bog. Uncle Downey was not in it.

'Where is he?' demanded Merkle.

'Over here, over here,' cried the impatient old man. 'I have your fool frog.'

They ploughed towards his voice, careful to avoid swampy patches.

'Seems all but impossible,' declared Sash. 'A place like this, only a frog jump from the heart of Manhattan. Looks almost prehistoric.'

'It is,' said Linda. 'This vast bog is where Uncle Downey does most of his duck research.'

They rounded a bend in the swamp to face the apartment-sized frog, in front of which stood Linda's uncle with a small gold whistle.

'What's he going to do?' queried Sash.

Linda shook her head in bewilderment.

Merkle advanced with his revolver at the ready.

'Stay back!' rasped the old man. 'He's fast with his tongue. Let me handle this. Back, back, back!'

They retreated a few steps, watching the big frog.

It was impressive. Its huge bulbous eyes blinked vacantly and its distended throat pulsed like an immense heart. It was handsomely spotted.

'Be careful, Uncle Downey,' warned Linda.

Her uncle ignored her, bringing the whistle to his lips. He blew soft tweeting sounds. The frog's eyes began to go sleepy.

'Oh, now I see,' said Linda. 'Uncle Downey is lulling it into a comatose state. His tiny golden whistle is obviously ultrasonic, and we are hearing only the low register.'

'Great!' said Merkle. 'He's *some* old gentleman!'

Uncle Downey swung grumpily around to face them. 'Stop your blather! You'll ruin everything, ruin it all.'

The frog suddenly shifted, snaked out a long tongue, and

snapped Uncle Downey off the ground and into its mouth. One swallow and the cranky eccentric was gone, whistle, raincoat, thick eyeglasses and all.

'Boy!' marvelled Sash. 'He was right. That is one *fast* tongue!'

'I could whack a few .38 slugs into its belly,' Merkle suggested.

Linda sighed. 'A pointless display of gunfire won't bring Uncle Downey back.'

'She's right, chief,' Sash agreed. 'But what now?'

'We leave the big devil for the present,' said Dave Merkle, reluctantly holstering his custom-grip revolver. 'If we're lucky he may just stay in this area looking for more growth pellets. Let's head back to Washington.'

Linda picked up her late uncle's fallen umbrella and followed them towards the waiting battery car.

Five-star General Jordan Fielding Elliott rapped his maple map pointer smartly against his booted leg. 'Then, as I understand it, what we basically have here is a giant hop-toad loose in the Catskills?'

Merkle nodded. 'That's right, General Elliott.'

'Call me General Fielding. I never use the Elliott, except for paper work.'

'Right,' said Merkle.

'And the toad *is* dangerous?'

'Indeed,' said Linda, 'it is—having eaten, at the very least, a Corvette driver named Betts, and my Uncle Downey. But we must not mix toads with frogs. The creature we're dealing with in this case is a common bullfrog, though greatly enlarged.'

'Thank you, Miss Pinning,' said the general. 'I'll make a note of that.' He turned to a small, moustached assistant. 'Lights, if you please.'

The room darkened as the people in the small projection area settled into their chairs. In addition to Fielding and his aide, several high-ranking government officials were in attendance. 'I love a good movie,' one of them said.

A flickering, slightly off-focus 8 mm film filled one corner of the forward screen, showing dozens of frogs leaping and sunning themselves. Linda Pinning calmly provided the narration.

'As you will see in this simple nature film, taken by my late Uncle Downey at Sleepy Hollow, the bullfrog, or *Rana catesbeiana,* is the most carnivorous of the species. Its natural diet consists of earthworms, spiders, and other insects, although it has been known to occasionally devour waterfowl and small chickens.'

'Alarming!' a Congressman muttered in the darkness.

'The *Rana catesbeiana* croaks loudest of the frog family, and is particularly fond of cool, damp places. Thus, its swamp home in the Catskills is ideal and characteristic.'

The film snapped to white, and Linda accepted a spatter of applause.

Cigars and pipes were lighted as Dave Merkle asked the general what he planned to do.

'Simple,' Fielding smiled, adjusting a lopsided campaign ribbon. 'We despatch a whirlybird and some nets and we capture the big toad and—'

'Frog,' said Linda.

'We capture the damn thing is all! Stick it in a zoo. Simple. That's how things work at my end of the hall.'

Nods all around.

The plan sounded fine.

They tried netting the frog.

They tried bombing the frog.

They tried cannons and tank guns and laser fire.

With negative results.

For one thing, the frog kept hopping in odd directions, and they couldn't keep up with it. The situation became vital when it flattened the President's summer house in San Clemente. (It had also eaten a considerable number of people, including two prominent screen personalities, and the public was aroused.)

General Fielding arranged an emergency Pentagon session

with full Congressional backing in order to make an important announcement.

'We are faced,' he said, 'with what can only be termed a mounting dilemma.' He turned to Linda. 'Miss Pinning, would you fill the folks in on the latest?'

'Of course,' she said. 'As you may have surmised from recent reports, the frog has now *doubled* in size since it was first noted in the Catskills. We do not know exactly why the cell structure, nervous system and body tissues of the *Rana catesbeiana* are receptive to erratic or uncontrolled growth, but—regretfully—my late Uncle Downey's experimental pellets could not have affected any other natural creature to this degree.'

'Will the son of a bitch keep growing?' asked a Nebraska senator.

'I'm very much afraid so,' Linda replied. 'But the rate is uncertain.'

A rumble of discontent swept the room.

Fielding rapped the lectern sharply with his maple map stick. 'Folks we have no choice. I declare this project on Red Alert!'

'What does that mean?' asked Dave Merkle.

'It means I have White House authority to order the use of a hitherto top-secret weapon.' He measured the crowd with hard eyes. 'You might even call it America's *ultimate* weapon.'

Excited murmuring.

Fielding turned back to the girl. 'Miss Pinning, is there some way we could get the frog to swallow a fairly large quantity of metallic substances?'

Linda raised an eyebrow. 'I think he already has. Along with his unfortunate victims, he's swallowed rings, wrist watches, tie clips, fountain pens, belt buckles, eye-glasses, gold fillings, keys, coins, metal shoe laces ...'

Fielding shook his head. 'What about Corvettes? He likes those, doesn't he?'

'He's swallowed three of them over the past month,' Eldon volunteered.

'Right! Then we feed him all the Corvettes he can eat. And when he's got a bellyful, we go on green.' He pointed to his moustached aide. 'Round up a couple dozen Corvettes.'

'New or used?'

'Forget the vintage,' roared Fielding.

'He seemed to like new ones,' Sash put in. 'They slide down easier.'

'All right, nothing older than 1980 but hurry. Get those cars to that frog, pronto!'

It was dubbed Operation Sky Pole for obvious reasons—it *was* a pole, and it went into the sky. Based under the Texas prairie, it rose at the touch of a button, not unlike a giant automobile radio antenna, to a height of three miles. Topping it were twin metal globes with high-voltage electricity dancing between them, designed to attract any flying metallic object within 2500 miles. The basic idea, as Fielding explained it, was that an enemy guided missile approaching the U.S. would be drawn into the pole's magnetic field and instantly disintegrated by awesomely powerful electronic forces.

'Our frog, full of Corvettes, will be sucked in and totally destroyed,' declared Fielding from his underground command post near Waco.

The bunker was awash in dignitaries.

'Where's the creature now?' asked Merkle.

'Dozing on the flats a few miles from Salt Lake City. He ate every Corvette we offered him—and finished off with a Land Rover. Oh, he's *full* of metal, all right! Once he's airborne, we activate the pole and watch the fireworks. Be like shooting ducks in a barrel.'

'It's fish,' Linda corrected. 'Fish in a barrel.'

'Never mind that,' Fielding snapped. 'You'll see what I mean.'

The general, wearing his full-dress uniform, walked to a wall of blinking red and green lights. He checked a radar screen. 'Everything is one hundred percent up to date here,' he said proudly. 'We'll be able to track our spotted friend

A-OK all the way from Salt Lake.'

'How do you plan to get him to jump?' Eldon wanted to know. 'Sometimes he just snoozes for days. And weighted down the way he is . . .'

'That's being taken care of,' Fielding assured him. 'Able Company will lob hand grenades at his stomach. He just *hates* that. He'll jump out of sheer annoyance.'

They crowded closer to the radar screen.

'Ready, sir?' asked the moustached aide.

'Lob!' shouted Fielding.

The aide repeated the order to lob into a field telephone.

Fielding checked his wristwatch. 'The big countdown begins, gentlemen! In ten seconds, that treacherous demon frog will be just so many spotted atoms floating in the void.'

A blip began moving on the screen.

'He's in the air, General Elliott!' the aide squealed.

'It's Fielding! I never use Elliott, you damn fool. Confound you, now I've lost the count!'

'. . . six, five, four,' offered Dave Merkle.

'Yes! . . . three, two, *one* . . . Watch this! He's—'

A ground-quaking explosion. Dust and chunks of loosened concrete rained down.

All the red and green lights went out.

'What the hell's happened?' gasped the general, groping for his maple map stick on the floor of the darkened bunker.

'Apparently, sir, he struck the pole with one of his horny toes,' reported the shaky voice of the moustached aide. 'Our balls were dislodged—and the whole thing fell down on Waxahachie.'

'This is going to look terrible on my record,' moaned Fielding.

'Let's get out of here,' said Dave Merkle.

Linda was gone when the smoke cleared at ground level.

Merkle looked concerned. 'Do you think she's trapped below?'

'No, sir, she isn't,' Fielding's aide stated. 'I just observed

Miss Pinning drive off in a field utility truck, headed due south.'

'That's where the frog landed,' declared Sash.

'She said something about coming to grips with her uncle's problem.'

Merkle prodded Sash towards an empty jeep. 'She's going to do something rash, Eldon, I'm certain of that. Let's see if we can catch her.' He knuckled his forehead. 'You drive. I have an awful headache.'

When Merkle and Sash caught up with Linda she was standing close to the mammoth frog, holding on to a small perforated cardboard box which she'd removed from her purse.

'Keep back,' she told them. 'He's stunned, but still quite dangerous.'

The two men remained near the jeep, nervously eyeing the spotted giant. It squatted, dazed, on the desert floor, blinking stupidly.

Linda took off the lid and held the box aloft.

A wet, melancholy croak issued from the interior.

The huge frog ceased blinking. Its throat began a rapid pulsation.

It croaked deafeningly.

'I need a jet,' Linda told Merkle, running towards him, the box in her hand. 'Where can I borrow a jet?'

'There's one back at Waco Field,' Merkle said, 'but I don't think they'll let you use it.'

She vaulted in the jeep. 'Head for it! He'll be following us.'

As Eldon Sash gunned away in a scattering of gravel, the frog attempted to leap after them (overshooting by several miles.

'My God!' breathed Sash. 'What have you done to him?'

'Talking is superfluous. Just get us to that jet!'

At the airport, Linda convinced a bewildered Fielding that she was a qualified pilot. 'Science and toe-dancing aren't my *only* talents!'

In the air, with Linda at the controls, Fielding demanded

to know what the hell was going on. Merkle and Sash looked blank.

Also frightened.

Because the frog was still following them.

'Even with his substantial jump range, we can keep ahead of him,' Linda said brightly. 'Boys, this is the last lap. The chequered flag's in sight.'

The small cardboard box rested on the seat beside her.

Near Sleepy Hollow, the jet swept downward, skimmed the trees with a great slicing roar, and landed bumpily on a deserted stretch of New York highway.

'Everyone out!' Linda shouted. 'He'll be here any minute, and we need to be properly positioned.'

'For what?' demanded Fielding. 'Positioned for *what?*' Sweat seeded his weak upper lip and his braided hat was on crooked.

Linda scampered across the highway into the woods, still clutching the box. The others trudged after her.

At the edge of the vast bog she paused, opened the lid, and a tiny green bullfrog flopped out.

'There!' said Linda triumphantly.

A trumpet croak in the sky.

Down came the immense spotted giant.

It landed, with a wet smack, in the exact centre of the bog.

Within moments, the quicksand had sucked it under.

'Sex did the job,' said Linda.

'Explain yourself, Miss Pinning!' The general was still confused, and the front of his full-dress uniform was splashed with swamp mud.

'There is one call no creature can resist.'

'And that is?' prompted Sash.

'The mating call,' she said, giving Dave Merkle a knowing smile.

The tiny female frog from the box hopped over his left foot.

It croaked sweetly.

ONE OF THOSE DAYS

I knew it was going to be one of those days when I heard a blue-and-yellow butterfly humming *Si, mi chiamano Mimi*, my favourite aria from *La Bohème*. I was weeding the garden when the papery insect fluttered by, humming beautifully.

I got up, put aside my garden tools and went into the house to dress. I would see my psychoanalyst at once.

Neglecting my cane and spats, I snapped an old homburg on my head and aimed for Dr. Mellowthin's office in downtown Los Angeles.

Several disturbing things happened to me on the way ...

First of all, a large stippled Tomcat darted out of an alley directly after I'd stepped from the bus. The cat was on its hind legs and carried a bundle of frothy pink blanketting in its front paws. It looked desperate.

'Gangway!' shouted the cat. 'Baby! Live baby here! Clear back. BACK for the baby!'

Then it was gone, having dipped cat-quick across the street, losing itself in heavy traffic. Upon drawing in a deep lungful of air, smog-laden but steadying, I resumed my brisk pace towards Dr. Mellowthin's office.

As I passed a familiar apartment house a third-storey window opened and Wally Jenks popped his head over the sill and called down to me. 'Hi,' yelled Wally. 'C'mon up for a little drinkie.'

I shaded my eyes to get a clearer look at him. 'Hi, Jenks!' I yelled back, and we both grinned foolishly at the old play on words. 'On my way to Mellowthin's.'

'Appointment?' he queried.

'Spur of the moment,' I replied.

'Then time's no problem. Up you come, old dads, or I shan't forgive you.'

I sighed and entered the building. Jenks was in 3G, and I decided to use the stairs. Elevators trap you. As I reached the second-floor landing I obeyed an irresistible urge to bend down and place my ear close to the base of the wall near the floor.

'Are you mice still *in* there?' I shouted.

To which a thousand tiny musical Disney-voices shot back: 'Damned *right* we are!'

I shrugged, adjusted my homburg, and continued my upward climb. Jenks met me at the door with a dry martini.

'Thanks,' I said, sipping. As usual, it was superb. Old Wally knew his martinis.

'Well,' he said, all cheer, 'how goes?'

'Badsville,' I answered. 'Care to hear?'

'By all means. Unburden.'

We sat down, facing one another across the tastefully furnished room. I sipped the martini and told Wally about things. 'This morning, bout forty minutes ago, I heard a butterfly humming Puccini. Then I saw a cat carrying what I can only assume was a live baby.'

'Human?'

'Don't know. Could have been a cat baby.'

'Cat say anything?'

'He shouted "Gangway!"'

'Proceed.'

'Then—on the way upstairs—I had a brief conversational exchange with at least a thousand mice.'

'In the walls?'

'Where else?'

'Finish your drinkie,' said Jenks, finishing his.

I did so.

'Nother?' he asked.

'Nope. Gotta be trotting. I'm in for a mental purge.'

'Well, I wouldn't worry too much,' he assured me. 'Humming insects, talking felines and odd-ball answering mice are admittedly upsetting. But... there *are* stranger things in this man's world.'

I looked over at him. And knew he was correct—for old Wally Jenks had turned into a loose-pelted brown camel with twin humps, all stained and worn-looking at the tops.

I swallowed.

'See you,' I said.

Wally grinned, or rather the camel did, and it was awful. Long, cracked yellow teeth like old carnival dishes inside his black gums. I gave a nervous little half-wave, and moved for the door. One final glance over my shoulder at old Jenks verified the fact that he was still grinning at me with those big wet desert-red eyes of his.

Back on the street I quickened my stride, anxious now to reach Mellowthin and render a full account of the day's events. Only a half-block to go.

Then a policeman stopped me. He was all sweaty inside his tight uniform, and his face was dark with hatred.

'Thought you was the wise one, eh, Mugger?' he rasped in a venom-filled voice. 'Thought you could give John Law the finger?'

'But, officer, I don't—'

'Come right along, Mugger. We got special cages for the likes 'a you.' He was about to snap a pair of silver cuffs to my wrists when I put a quick knee to his vitals and rabbit-punched him on the way down. Then I grabbed his revolver.

'Here!' I shouted to several passers-by. 'This man is a fraud. Killed a cop to get this rig. He's a swine of the worst sort. Record as long as your arm. Blackmail, rape, arson, autotheft, kidnapping, grand larceny, wife-beating and petty pilfering. You name it, he's done it!'

I thrust the revolver at a wide-eyed, trembling woman. 'Take this weapon, lady. If he makes a funny move, shoot to kill!'

She aimed the gun at the stunned policeman, who was only now getting his breath. He attempted to rise.

'OOPS!' I yelled, 'he's going for a knife. Let him have it—NOW!'

The trembling woman shut both eyes and pulled the trigger. The cop pitched forward on his face, stone dead.

'May heaven forgive you,' I moaned, backing away. 'You've murdered an officer of the law, a defender of public morals ... May heaven be merciful!'

The woman flapped off. She had turned into a heavy-billed pelican. The policeman had become a fat-bellied seal with flippers, but he was still dead.

Hurrying, and somewhat depressed, I entered Dr. Mellowthin's office and told the girl at the desk it was an emergency.

'You may go right in,' she told me. 'The doctor will see you immediately.'

In another moment I was pumping Mellowthin's hand.

'Sit down, boy,' he told me. 'So ... we've got our little complications again today, have we?'

'Sure have,' I said, pocketing one of his cigars. I noticed that it was stale.

'Care to essay the couch?'

I slid on to the rich dark leather and closed my eyes.

'Now—tell me all about it.'

'First a butterfly sang *La Bohème*, or hummed it rather. Then a Tomcat shot out of an alley with a baby in its paws. Then some mice in an apartment house yelled back at me. Then one of my oldest and dearest friends turned into a camel.'

'One hump or two?' asked Mellowthin.

'Two,' I said. 'Large and scruffy and all worn at the tops.'

'Anything else?'

'Then a big, pseudo-English cop stopped me. His dialogue was fantastic. Called me Mugger. Said I was fit for a cage. Started to put cuffs on me. I kneed him in the kishkas and gave his gun to a nice trembly lady who shot him. Then she turned into a pelican and flapped off, and he turned into a seal with flippers. Then I came here.'

I opened my eyes and sat up.

I stared at Dr. Mellowthin.

'What's the matter?' he asked, somewhat uneasily.

'Well ...' I said, 'to begin with you have large brown, sad looking, liquidy eyes.'

'And?'

'And I bet your nose is cold!' I grinned.

'Anything else?'

'Not really.'

'What about my overall appearance?'

'Well, of course you're covered with long black shaggy hair, even down to the tips of your floppy ears.'

A moment of strained silence.

'Can you do tricks?' I asked.

'A few,' Mellowthin replied uncomfortably.

'Roll over!' I commanded.

He did.

'Play dead!'

His liquidy eyes rolled up white and his long pink tongue lolled loosely from his jaws.

'Good doggie,' I said. 'Nice doggie.'

'Woof,' barked Dr. Mellowthin softly, wagging his tail.

Putting on my hat I tossed him a bone I'd saved from the garden and left his office.

There was absolutely no getting around it.

This was simply one of those days.

TILDY

Although the passenger rocket's tumultuous departure seemed to delight her new husband, Tildy Perchall found Blast-Off a singularly unpleasant experience.

'Well, Til, how do you feel, eh?' Phineas asked as they shot away from Earth. He grinned broadly. 'Now, wasn't that *something*?'

'I feel like an elephant sat on my chest,' she said.

'Boy, they really sparkle out there, don't they?' enthused Phineas, pressing his nose against the port and squinting at the stars. 'I mean they *glitter*!'

Tildy stared unhappily at the man she had so recently married; at his scratchy moustache like a patch of brown weed under his long nose; at his small pig eyes and disappointing ears; and at the sparse beginnings of a beard on his weak, recessive chin.

Phineas was not only a bore, she reluctantly admitted, but he was positively *ugly*! Still, Tildy knew she had no business being particular.

Sadly, she examined her own reflection in the dark port glass. Good features, basically. Attractive white teeth, naturally curly blonde hair, soft doe eyes and full lips. Framed in the liquid depths of the port, her face was beautiful—as a peach swollen with summer juices is beautiful.

Then she looked down. The rest of her body flowed beneath like a pink sea and she told herself, once again, that considering her incredible poundage she was lucky to have landed even Phineas in the competitive game of Man-catching.

Sighing, she studied the other passengers. Waspish school teachers on vacation. Fox-faced salesmen and ulcered business moguls. The fact that they were all equally unattractive comforted her somewhat.

'Are you *sure* the moon is warm?' she asked Phineas. 'I could just bet it isn't. Ellie Fullbrick says it just gets terribly awfully cold up there at night. She says that if—'

'You can forget the moon,' Phineas Perchall announced. 'Utterly dismiss its depressingly pocked face from your mind. We are not headed for the moon at all.'

Tildy was confused. She blinked. 'Then—where *are* we going?'

'Surprise!' smiled Phineas. 'Idea came to me right in the middle of *Ape, Fruitfly And You*. I suddenly realized how stagnant, how dormant and suffocating life has been, how we all subconsciously yearn to burst our fetters and unite with the animal kingdom.'

'But, Phineas ...'

'Boliver Chadwick gave me this colossal idea. Fellow who wrote the book. Anthropologist, you know. Big. Over two hundred pounds. Full of odd facts. Knows all about the Hawk Indians, for example.'

'But, what have the Hawk Indians to do with our honeymoon?'

'At the end of chapter fourteen my subconscious whispered,' Phineas went on, his voice excited and high. 'Why spend our honeymoon in lacklustre surroundings? The Moon is old hat; Mars is a bore. But, ah, what of the Evening Star? What of Venus? Why not spend our honeymoon running free and unbridled like young gazelles in the jungles of Venus? Imagine, two full weeks in the lap of the primitive!'

Tildy thought of a camping trip she'd once taken as a Brownie. Out in the wind, chilled and uncomfortable, rained on and bitten by insects which seemed to find her ample flesh a special culinary delight. 'It rains on Venus,' she protested. 'I read about it. Terrible rain most of the time.'

'Rain is a fine unbridled process—a letting-down, as it were, of Nature's hair—a pouring forth of her crystal gifts!'

'Bugs,' Tildy moaned. 'There must be all kinds of new bugs up there. We could be stung to death—or even eaten alive.'

'Nonsense. Chadwick was absolutely right when he wrote: "Life's dull plodding must occasionally be enlivened by the extraordinary."'

Tildy felt herself going under in the torrential sea of her husband's argument. Phineas swept on.

'Adventure is what we're after. The challenge of the great outdoors. The clash of fang against fang!'

Tildy imagined an alien fang embedded in her pink leg. She moaned softly. 'But, Phineas, your job. We simply can't be going all the way to Venus!'

'Of course we can,' he grinned. 'This ship is equipped with the Shockley Solardrive Unit. Why, we're halfway there already. Gad, I feel seventeen again!'

Tildy sighed, resigned herself, and said nothing.

Free Fall proved to be immeasurably entertaining. Tildy adored drifting about the cabin, free of gravity, propelling herself, with a single neat fingerjab, from wall to wall. Looking down at her solid rotundity, airborne and light as thistle, she was continually amazed that so much of her managed to stay up there, suspended above the seats.

Drifting and swirling like a lazy feather, she imagined herself a candle-thin fashion model, swathed in ermine and silk, posing for exclusive magazines. She could almost feel the looped pearls about her throat.

And then Phineas spoiled it all.

Swimming into the centre of the cabin, he began to sing lustily. 'Row, row, row your boat, gently down the stream ... merrily, merrily, merrily, merrily, life is but a dream ...'

A woman with hair like streaming confetti propelled herself up to join in the chorus. A space salesman added his nasal twang to the din as the entire cabin boomed with song.

Tildy floated wearily back to her seat, crushed in a winepress of merrilys. She strapped herself in and closed her eyes against the sight of Phineas, whose open mouth somehow resembled a decorated Easter egg.

Bells, buzzers, flashing lights, released pressures—and a final jarring thump.

'Well, kid,' said Phineas, smacking his palms together, 'we're down.'

'That was a terrible landing,' Tildy said, after the solar engines had stilled. 'I must have broken something.' She felt gingerly of her deep-sunk bones.

'Nonsense. Let us disembark to greet a new world. Old Mother Earth is nothing more than a single lost grain of sand on the trackless beach of the Universe. Venus, the Evening Star, bids us welcome!'

Outside the rocket, the rain spatted down from a leaden sky. Tildy gazed at the soaked jungle rising in a leafy tide beyond the perimeter of the landing area. Under the beating rain the trees lashed and twisted; odd web-leafed bushes glinted balefully; furry creatures whipped bullet-quick through matted undergrowth.

Tildy shuddered.

She turned to face a hurrying little man with a basket on his arm. Smiling, he came trotting forward to meet them as they descended from the rocket with the other passengers.

From the basket, the little man dropped wreaths over each of the female visitors. He then led them towards the depot—an immense, bubble-like structure at the clearing's edge.

Phineas took Tildy immediately to the main information desk.

'We intend to live as our primitive forefathers lived before us,' he announced to the slim young man behind the desk, 'shorn of artificial luxuries and stripped to essentials.'

The clerk squinted at Phineas.

'I want all the available information pertaining to big-game hunting,' Phineas said. 'We've got to live by our wits out there you know.'

'Out *where?*' asked the clerk.

'In the bush, boy. The untrammelled wilderness.'

'Look, mister, I think you've got the wrong planet.'

'But the folders *distinctly* mentioned a glorious life in the jungles!' He waved a gaudy pamphlet in the clerk's face.

'They mean the two square miles of jungle under the Dome,' replied the youth. 'A breathable atmosphere is maintained and all activities are safely-supervised. No hunting allowed.'

'Great heaven, boy, do you mean to tell me that a raw, primitive, jungle existence is impossible?'

'All I go by are the rules, mister. And the rules say that all tourists stay *under* the Dome.'

'They's *one* man what ain't under no gawdam dome,' rasped an ancient voice. 'They's one feller out there an' *he* damwell ain't safety-supervised!'

A wizened old Spacer with a face like a dry river bed stood near the desk. A ragged uniform hung from his withered stick body.

The clerk scowled and shook his head. 'Don't pay any attention to old Cooney. Everyone knows he's space happy.'

Phineas peered into a leathery, lined face. 'You mean that there's a human being living out there—in the bush?'

'Dang right I do!'

'He believes in the White God legend,' growled the clerk.

'Some crazy story they tell of a tall white God who lives in the heart of the jungle.'

Cooney stamped his foot. 'I tellya I *seed* him oncet meself! Plain as day, he was. Seed him down in a clean stretch a ground, a clearin' it was, when I flew the Lucy Mae over. Breathin' easy as ya please—and without no space helmick neither!'

'Why, Tildy!' exclaimed Phineas, turning to his wife. 'If this old fellow speaks truth can't you see what it means? If I can capture this God; bring him back to civilization, our fortunes will be made!'

'But, Phineas, our honeymoon ...'

'We'll make it a two-in-one-trip. A honeymoon and a hunting expedition.'

'Waal, he's out thar right enough,' spat the old man. 'An' fer grub an' keep and drinkin' likker, I'll lead ya right ta that clearin' by dad!'

'Oh, Tildy, is this not the kind of adventure to stir a man's blood? A rough shoot, a ready quest.' He turned to the clerk. 'Now, boy, I'll need a safari and supplies.'

'Look, mister, it's forbidden in the rules. It would take Mr. Spearblock himself to change the rules and he—'

'Tut,' said Phineas acidly. 'Lead the way to this Spearblock. I'll state my case in the kind of plain language I'm sure he understands.' Behind his cupped palm he whispered to Tildy. 'Money talks, my love, and we've *your* savings to speak for us!'

Planetary Affairs Chief R. W. Spearblock tipped far back in his swivel-chair and thoughtfully laid the orange length of a Ticonderoga earth pencil along his richly veined nose. 'A highly unusual request, Mr. Perchall. Most unusual indeed.'

'Shall we say ...' Phineas leaned forward, eyes slitted, 'one thousand dollars for your services?'

'Ah,' Mr. Spearblock placed a tiny scented mint on the pink ledge of his tongue and smiled. 'A bargain, sir. Of course you must realize that I cannot assume any responsibility as to your safety. But you shall have your safari and supplies.'

'But—what about the natives?' asked Tildy. 'Will they like the idea of our tramping around in their jungle?'

Spearblock pressed a small button on his desk. 'I have summoned Matoosh to act in your behalf. He is himself a native and only recently offered to aid us in native affairs. You'll find him capable and trustworthy, I'm sure.'

A second later the door opened and the Venusian glided in. He was nine feet tall with a body like an elongated basketball, six green tentacles and a pair of sad eyes on stalks. He floated about a foot above the floor.

'Good afternoon, Matoosh.'

'Afternoon, sir. I was reading when you buzzed.'

'Something good?'

'Plato, sir.'

'I'm sorry, Matoosh.'

'Quite all right, sir. I marked my place.'

After this friendly exchange Spearblock introduced the Perchalls. Matoosh bowed gravely to each of them; and Tildy was surprised to find that the alien was not actually repulsive to her. Odd, certainly, but not repulsive.

'I hope you'll make it clear to your people that we mean them no harm,' said Phineas.

'Naturally, sir.'

'Your safari will be ready to leave at sunrise tomorrow,' Spearblock told them. 'Matoosh will accompany you to your destination.'

The alien bowed once more to each of them, and glided out of the room.

At least he's very polite, thought Tildy, watching the door close behind him.

The safari set out at the precise crack of dawn. Matoosh, Phineas, Tildy and the old space rat, Cooney, took the lead, followed by a line of twenty Earth bearers, supplies carefully balanced on their shining space helmets.

Tildy had been given a case of *Swanongi* juice by Matoosh, who told her it would do marvels for her weight. The fact that she would be able to shed some excess poundage helped considerably to dispel much of the gloom originally associated with the safari. Tildy was even able to appreciate the strange beauty of the Venusian jungle.

During the night the rain had stopped and a hot, lemon-yellow sun swelled huge and heavy over the misted foliage. The jungle was a blaze of amazing colours, and the webbed leaves sparkled and shone.

Tildy could hear the sweet early-morning song of birds; and the small furry animals which scampered out of her path reminded her of the pet squirrels she used to feed in her yard back home, with their plump tummies and toy-button eyes.

As the day wore on, however, the jungle began to steam under the high-riding sun. Gasping inside her helmet, Tildy staggered up to Matoosh at the noon halt.

'The jungle is like an oven,' she complained. 'The heat is just *awful*!'

'Might I then, madam, offer a simple suggestion?'

'Certainly.'

The alien folded four of his tentacles behind his back. 'I suggest the immediate removal of that which you term your girdle.'

Tildy flushed angrily. 'I ought to slap your face!'

'I have no face,' Matoosh said truthfully.

'How dare you suggest such a—a *personal* thing!'

'The incredible garment is wholly unnecessary. It merely binds and constricts.'

'I'd look a sight,' Tildy said, attempting to smooth the lumpy ridge of girdle at her waist.

'In the jungle, comfort is a prime requisite. And I fail to see how one can be comfortable in an Earth girdle.'

With that he bowed and ballooned gently away.

'Good Lord!' exclaimed Phineas on the second day's

march. 'How can you go along humming in this fantastic heat, Matilda?'

Tildy smiled shyly, eyes downcast. 'I—I just got rid of things. I just don't think you should fight Venus. It's really rather *nice*.'

Phineas trudged on in silence. With each step his heavy pack seemed to press him deeper into the soft ground.

'You're carrying way too much,' Tildy told him. 'Why did you have to drag along that full set of Chadwick?'

Phineas halted, glaring at his wife. 'Now where, may I ask, would we be on a trip of this kind without Chadwick's *The Aboriginal And What Makes Him Tick*? When we find this wild devil we'll have to deal with him intelligently. And that is where Chadwick shines! The man is an absolute genius when it comes to the savage mind.'

'Well,' said Tildy, 'I do hope you're right.'

'My back is killing me,' groaned Phineas on the third day. 'I simply cannot voyage another mile.'

'I feel wonderful,' smiled Tildy. 'I've lost three pounds a day since Matoosh gave me that wonderful *Swanongi* juice!'

'Yowth!' Phineas began hopping about on one foot.

'What's wrong now?'

'Thorn. Right in my big toe. *Damn* these thorn bushes!'

'You ought to watch where you step. I always watch where I'm walking.'

She knelt beside him and helped him off with his boot. 'Quit squirming,' she demanded, 'and I'll bandage it.'

In the camp that evening Matoosh glided up to Phineas.

'The bearers, sir.'

'What about them?'

'They are restive and fearful. I overhead their mutterings.'

'What do they fear?' asked Phineas.

'The curse of the White God, sir. I'm very much afraid they are prone to dark imaginings.'

'I'm not a well man, Matoosh, and I simply cannot concern myself with such idiotic business. Have old Cooney talk to them. Tell him to tell them, for Lord's sake, that everything is hunky dory.'

'I shall do my best, sir.' Matoosh faded quietly into the dark.

'I'm struck!' shouted Phineas on the morning of the fourth day. 'My hand is paralysed!'

'Let me see it,' said Tildy. 'Maybe you just scratched yourself.'

'Allow me to know when I've been bitten,' snapped Phineas. 'One of these confounded Venusian pests sank a fang in my baby finger. Poisoned it, most likely.'

'Well, you haven't been using the *Punogee* oil Matoosh gave us. No wonder things bit you. Now, calm down. Here's Matoosh.'

'Relatively harmless, sir,' declared the green Venusian, hovering professionally over the injured digit. 'Your finger will swell, but by the week's end you'll feel no ill effects.'

Tildy sighed and reached for the bandages.

That night in camp Phineas resembled a snowfall. In addition to the bandaged thumb and foot, he now carried his left arm in a sling.

'That arm looks nasty,' Tildy commented, sipping a cup of hot cocoa in their pressurized tent.

Phineas emitted a half-sob and fell back on his pillow. 'The bone is undoubtedly splintered beyond repair. I'll be maimed for life.'

'You silly thing. You should have *seen* that animal trap. I did, and missed it with no trouble. Have some cocoa?'

'Hell, no!' Phineas exploded. 'Hell, no, I won't have some cocoa! I'll die of thirst out here. I'll rot in this stinking jungle!' He was on his feet, arms flailing the air.

'Oh, sit down, Phineas, before you fall down. Remember, all this was your idea. You were the one who wanted to live in the lap of the primitive, to brave the trackless wild, to pit your strength against—'

'That's fine,' Phineas cut in furiously. 'Quote me. Fine! Throw the words in my face like old fish.'

Phineas suddenly peered at his wife, a strange new light in his eyes. He slowly extended a questing hand and prodded Tildy's waist. 'Matilda! You've taken off your girdle!'

'It was binding.'

'And—' He poked gingerly at her upper anatomy. 'I mean, you're not wearing a—'

'It constricted.'

'Good Lord!'

'I just—unbridled,' said Tildy. 'And I haven't felt this good in years. I have Matoosh to thank for it all. He's really a dear.'

And, picking up a copy of *Ape, Fruitfly And You*, she retired to her cot.

At the end of the fifth day's march, Phineas caught his left foot in a *Swanongi* root and sprained his ankle. He hobbled into camp on makeshift crutches.

'Damn this rotten bush country!' he gasped, tears in his eyes. 'It's absolutely destroying me. My battered carcass will soon be left for the—'

'Guess what, Phineas?' Tildy cut in. 'I've lost more weight! At least nine more pounds. Isn't it wonderful?'

'If the insects miss,' Phineas continued, 'if I survive the traps, the sun will get me. Bake me to the bone, cook me like a suckling pig. I'll be burned to an ash in this damned—'

'If I could lose three pounds a day for twenty-four days, then I'd weigh only a hundred and ten!'

The pressure-flap hissed and Matoosh glided into the tent. 'Beg pardon, sir, but the bearers have, as you say on Earth, flown the coop.'

Phineas blinked up at the alien. 'Do you mean to tell me that the ungrateful wretches have bolted camp?'

'Evidently they measured their pay against their superstition and the latter won out. However, the venerable Mr. Cooney is still with us.'

'How terrible!' exclaimed Tildy.

'Their action, I must admit, was not entirely without provocation.' Matoosh paused, and his eyes lowered. 'I am ashamed to report that some of my own people entered camp earlier this evening and quite dismembered their leader before I could intervene.'

'Great Scott! Then we're under attack!' roared Phineas.

Matoosh raised a calming tentacle. 'No need for alarm, sir. I was quite firm in cautioning my people against future indiscretions. We may, I assure you, proceed in perfect safety.'

'Thank you, Matoosh,' Tildy smiled. 'We're very lucky to have you with us.'

Before she went to sleep that night, Tildy wondered just why Matoosh took so much trouble to protect them. They were, in point of fact, trespassers. She had the feeling that a special reason existed to justify the alien's behaviour, and that she, personally, was involved.

At noon, on the sixth day, old Cooney sighted the clearing. 'By ginger!' he shouted, running ahead and pointing. 'Thar it be! Thar's the clearin' jes like I said.'

The matted jungle fell back to reveal a mile-wide stretch of lush, sun-bright grass, which rippled like a huge green flag under the fingering wind.

Phineas adjusted his eyes and made out a small, log-like structure at the far edge of the clearing. He swung triumphantly to his wife. 'Didn't I tell you he existed? There's his primitive home. Crude and rough-hewn. The mark of the savage.'

Tildy said nothing. She felt a strange excitement rising in her.

'Let me handle everything,' Phineas said. 'The proper approach must be made, the proper overtures of friendliness extended, just as Chadwick advises. I'll do all the talking.'

Matoosh drifted up to Tildy. 'Mr. Perchall seems very excited.'

'Yes,' she replied. 'It's a big day for Phineas.'

'It is a big day, certainly—but *not* for your husband.'

'Why—what do you mean, Matoosh?' she tried to read an expression into the featureless balloon head.

Matoosh flicked a casual tentacle. 'He is to return to Earth. You are to remain.'

'You mean stay here, on Venus, without my husband?'

But Matoosh did not answer. He moved away, towards the cabin.

'HALT!' screamed Phineas, gesturing wildly. *'I'm* to make first contact. Halt, you protoplasmic blob!'

Mattoosh continued. He reached the cabin airlock and waited. A hiss, a sigh of escaping air, and the door opened.

A blond giant stood on the threshold.

Tildy gasped. The white savage was the handsomest man she had ever seen. He towered well over six feet and wore what seemed to be a type of fringed-buckskin suit. A small oxygen mask covered his lower jaw—thus dispelling the 'helmetless God' legend. Under his curling gold hair, his blue eyes were deep and steady, his cheekbones high and finely moulded. To Tildy, even his not-too-large not-too-small ears were marvellous to behold.

His appearance occasioned a moment of awed silence. Then Phineas rushed forward, his right hand out, palm up, in the Chadwick-inspired gesture of good will. 'I bear greetings from Earth, the third planet,' he said, 'to you in the wilderness of Venus.'

The giant did not speak.

Phineas hesitated, then asked, 'Can—you—speak—English?'

The tall savage did not move. He was looking beyond Phineas.

He was looking at Tildy.

An odd, delicious tingle needled through her; she felt as light as foam as she walked slowly up to the big stranger. 'Hello,' she said softly, 'I'm Matilda Perchall.'

'Hello, my dear,' the tall man said in flawless English, his tone deep and gentle. 'I've been waiting for you.'

He turned majestically to Phineas.

'Matoosh will accompany you and Mr. Cooney back to the Dome. Return at once to Earth and forget you ever saw this woman. She is now mine. And please do not question my orders. If you do, I have the power to *force* you to obey them. I hope, for your sake, that I will not have to use that power. Now, go.'

Phineas paled, then recovered some of his initiative. 'What do you mean you've been *waiting* for my wife? Why, this is all fantastic and preposterous! You can't possibly mean that I—'

'GO!' The giant's voice was stern and his rigid arm pointed into the jungle. As Matoosh glided forward to the slack-jawed Phineas, the big man swept Tildy into his arms.

The cabin airlock hissed, sliding open to receive them. He carried her over the threshold.

Slowly he lowered her to the floor and drew off her helmet. Then he removed his own lower-face mask.

Tildy goose-pimpled. 'I am fat,' she said trembling.

'Here, with the help of *Swanongi* juice, you will soon become slim and beautiful.'

'I am married to Phineas.'

'He is a boob, an oaf. You never really loved him.'

'But, I—'

'Matoosh arranged it all. He knows me better than I know myself. I needed a woman to complete my life, and so he brought you to me. He looked beyond your plump exterior, Matilda, and he knew that I would love you. And I do. I most assuredly do.'

Tildy felt giddy; her heart was fluttering like a frantic bird. 'I—I love you also!' she told him. 'And your jacket photo certainly doesn't *begin* to do you justice!'

Boliver Chadwick smiled modestly, flicking a bit of dust from his buckskin suit. 'Jacket photos never do.'

He lit a great briar with a wooden stick match and puffed deeply, drawing the scented smoke into his lungs. 'Now I have all the things I need: my work, solitude, an outdoor paradise, and a fine woman.' He seated himself on a low couch and patted his knee. 'Come, my dear.'

Tildy blushed, sighed, goose-pimpled—and moved towards the lap of the primitive.

DEAD CALL

Len had been dead for a month when the phone rang.

Midnight. Cold in the house and me dragged up from sleep to answer the call. Helen gone for the weekend. Me, alone in the house. And the phone ringing ...

'Hello.'

'Hello, Frank.'

'Who is this?'

'You know *me*. It's Len ... ole Len Stiles.'

Cold. Deep and intense. The receiver dead-cold matter in my hand.

'Leonard Stiles died four weeks ago.'

'Four weeks, three days, two hours and twenty-seven minutes ago—to be exact.'

'I want to know who you are?'

A chuckle. The same dry chuckle I'd heard so many times.

'C'mon, ole buddy—after twenty years. Hell, you *know* me.'

'This is a damned poor joke!'

'No joke, Frank. You're there, alive. And I'm here, dead. And you know something, ole buddy ... I'm really *glad* I did it.'

'Did ... what?'

'Killed myself. Because ... death is just what I hoped it would be. Beautiful ... grey ... quiet ... no pressures.'

'Len Stiles' death was an accident ... a concrete freeway barrier ... His car—'

'I *aimed* my car for that barrier,' the phone-voice told me. 'Pedal to the floor. Doing over ninety when I hit ... No accident, Frank.' The voice cold ... cold. 'I *wanted* to be dead. And no regrets.'

I tried to laugh, make light of this—matching his chuckle with my own. 'Dead men don't use telephones.'

'I'm not really using the phone, not in a physical sense. It's just that I chose to contact you this way. You might say it's a matter of "psychic electricity". As a detached spirit I'm able to align my cosmic vibrations to match the vibrations of this power line. Simple, really.'

'Sure. A snap. Nothing to it.'

'Naturally, you're sceptical. I expected you to be. But ... listen carefully to me, Frank.'

And I listened—with the phone gripped in my hand in that cold night house—as the voice told me things that *only* Len could know ... intimate details of shared experiences extending back through two decades. And when he'd finished I was certain of one thing:

He *was* Len Stiles.

'But, how ... I still don't ...'

'Think of this phone as a "medium"—a line of force through which I can bridge the gap between us.' The dry chuckle again. 'Hell, you gotta admit it beats holding hands around a table in the dark—yet the principle is the same.'

I'd been standing by my desk, transfixed by the voice. Now I moved behind the desk, sat down, trying to absorb this dark miracle. My muscles were wire-taut, my fingers cramped about the black receiver. I dragged in a slow breath, the night dampness of the room pressing at me.

'All right ... I don't ... believe in ghosts, don't ... pretend to understand any of this, but ... I'll accept it. I *must* accept it.'

'I'm glad, Frank—because it's important that we talk.' A long moment of hesitation. Then the voice, lower now, softer. 'I know how lousy things have been, ole buddy.'

'What do you mean?'

'I just know how things are going for you. And ... I want to help. As your friend, I want you to know that I understand.'

'Well ... I'm really not ...'

'You've been feeling bad, haven't you? Kind of "down", right?'

'Yeah ... a little, I guess.'

'And I don't blame you. You've got reasons. Lots of reasons. For one ... there's your money problem.'

'I'm expecting a raise. Shendorf promised me one—within the next few weeks.'

'You won't get it, Frank. I *know*. He's lying to you. Right now, at this moment, he's looking for a man to replace you at the company. Shendorf's planning to fire you.'

'He never liked me ... We never got along from the day I walked into that office.'

'And your wife ... all the arguments you've been having with her lately ... It's a pattern, Frank. Your marriage is all over. Helen's going to ask you for a divorce. She's in love with another man.'

'*Who*, dammit? What's his name?'

'You don't know him. Wouldn't change things if you did. There's nothing you can do about it now. Helen just ... doesn't love you any more. These things happen to people.'

'We've been ... drifting apart for the last year—but I didn't know why. I had no idea that she ...'

'And then there's Jan. She's back on it, Frank. Only it's worse now. A lot worse.'

I knew what he meant—and the coldness raked along my body. Jan was nineteen, my oldest daughter—and she'd been into drugs for the past three years. But she'd promised to quit.

'What do you know about Jan? Tell me!'

'She's into the heavy stuff, Frank. She's hooked bad. It's too late for her.'

'What the hell are you saying?'

'I'm saying she's lost to you ... She's rejected you, and there's no reaching her. She *hates* you ... blames you for everything.'

'I won't *accept* that kind of blame! I did my best for her.'

'It wasn't enough, Frank. We both know that. You'll never see Jan again.'

The blackness was welling within me, a choking wave through my body.

'Listen to me, old buddy. Things are going to get worse, not better. I know. I went through my own kind of hell when I was alive.'

'I'll ... start over ... leave the city—go East, work with my brother in New York.'

'Your brother doesn't want you in his life. You'd be an intruder ... an alien. He never writes you, does he?'

'No, but that doesn't mean—'

'Not even a card last Christmas. No letters or calls. He doesn't *want* you with him, Frank, believe me.'

And then he began to tell me other things ... He began to talk about middle age and how it was too late now to make any kind of new beginning ... He spoke of disease ... loneliness ... of rejection and despair. And the blackness was complete.

'There's only one real solution to things, Frank—just *one*. That gun you keep in your desk upstairs. Use it, Frank. Use the gun.'

'I couldn't do that.'

'But why not? What other choice have you got? The solution is *there*. Go upstairs and use the gun. I'll be waiting for you afterwards. You won't be alone. It'll be like the old days ... we'll be together ... Death is beautiful, Frank. I *know*. Life is ugly, but death is beautiful. ... Use the gun, Frank ... the gun ... use the gun ... the gun ... the gun ...'

I've been dead for a month now, and Len was right. It's fine here. No pressures. No worries. Grey and quiet and beautiful ...

I know how lousy things have been going for you. And they *won't* get any better.

Isn't that your phone ringing?

Better answer it.

It's important that we talk.

'It's just around the next turn,' Rice said, peering from the tinted windows as the bullet-car skimmed over the warm summer streets of the city.

The vehicle slowed, took the long curve with fluid grace, and whispered to a stop. A silver door panel sighed back and Ted Rice stepped into the heat of morning. His suit-conditioner immediately circulated an inner breath of cool air to balance the rise in temperature.

'I won't need you for the rest of the day,' he told the car. 'I'll be walking home.'

'May I have your location number, sir, in case a member of the family should wish to contact you?'

'No, dammit, you may not!' This was Free-Day. He needn't tell the car anything. 'Go home.'

'Very well, sir.' The machine slid obediently from the kerb. Rice watched it glitter briefly, like a lake trout in the moving wash of morning traffic, and disappear.

On Free-Days he told the car what to do. No predetermined destinations. No predetermined activities. Today the bars were open.

He intended to get very, very drunk.

On this morning, the sixth anniversary of his wife's death, Ted Rice had made two highly important decisions. He would quit his job, and he would turn Margaret in to Central Exchange. The job he hated, but it had been his life and quitting took courage. It meant beginning anew in an untried field and, at thirty-eight, that wasn't easy. Margaret he did not hate, finding it impossible to catologue his exact emotions where she was concerned. But his final decision to turn her in was the only one possible under the circumstances.

His reason for getting drunk, however, had nothing to do with his job or with Margaret. He was not, had never been, a drinking man. Intoxication was an anniversary ritual performed in memory of his late wife, Virginia. He exercised extreme care in his yearly choice of drinking quarters, avoiding pretentiousness because he wanted the surroundings to reflect his own inner loneliness.

Louie's Place was anything but pretentious. Ceaseless towellings had worn the bartop to a circular whiteness. The mirror behind it, in the shape of a giant passenger rocket, hung chipped and blackening at the edges. Even the mural, depicting Man's First Landing on the Red Planet, was dust-dimmed and faded, the paint cracking, peeling gradually away. The shabby stools fronting the bar were all unoccupied.

'Mornin',' greeted the bartender. Rice nodded, took a corner stool, and pressed the STRAIGHT WHISKY button. The drink glided into his hand and he downed it, grimacing.

'Ain't seen you around before on Free-Days,' the barman observed, swabbing idly at an already-dry glass ring. 'Just move inta th' neighbourhood?'

'I don't drink often,' Rice said, re-pressing the button.

'Wanna tell me about things?'

Rice shifted his attention from his shot glass to the man behind the bar. Beefy, slack-jawed, with a broken nose and a pair of watery, protuberant eyes over which lids folded like canvas sails. The face of mourning. The professional kindred soul, salaried receiver of woes and sad lament. Rice regarded him suspiciously, twirling the shot glass between thumb and forefinger.

'Well, Mac?'

'Turn around,' said Rice.

The big man grinned broadly, his solemn face splitting as though a paper knife had slit the skin across. 'Now I *know* you don't drink much. Believe me, I'm the real McCoy. In my racket, you have to be.'

'Around.'

Still grinning, the bartender complied. Law provided that evidence of a mechanical could not be concealed and there was no metal switch behind the man's right ear.

'Like I toldja, th' McCoy.'

'It's been a year,' Rice said, by way of apology. 'I wasn't sure they hadn't replaced you fellows, too.'

'Bars 'ud go broke if they did. Who wants to tell their troubles to a bunch a' springs an' cogs?'

Rice glanced at his wrist watch and thought of Margaret, standing in the living room of their modest home, a smile illuminating her delicate features. She had been standing now for fifteen hours, thirty-seven minutes—since he'd switched her off the previous evening in an angry display of temper.

'Six years ago today, my wife died in a copter crash,' Rice said, meeting the barman's sad eyes. 'I've put the memory of that crash away in the back of my mind and once each year I take it out and I remember.' He tipped the shot glass at a careful angle, holding it quite still, as though he might capture Virginia's tiny image there within the dark liquid, as a fly is caught in amber. 'I remember how she looked when they brought her up to the house, as if her bones had suddenly run wild under the skin, the way her face looked ... the face of someone I'd never met.'

Rice finished his fourth straight whisky, feeling it burn down through his body, loosening inner tensions, making it easier to say what he subconsciously *had* to say.

'That can be rough.' The big man looked wonderfully, professionally sympathetic, with those mournful red-rimmed eyes, which seemed about to flood into tears. 'Didja have any kids?'

'A boy, Jackie. He'll be nine this Game-Day. Lot like his mother. The other children, Timmy and Susan, are mechanicals. Got them after Virgie's death, when I bought Margaret.'

'Musta been tough on th' kid, losin' his real mother an' all.'

'Jackie doesn't remember much about Virgie. He was only three. Fact is, I've been half a stranger to him myself, on the road most of the year. Margaret's all right, I suppose, but she doesn't think the way you and I do.'

'How come you stuck yourself with this Margaret?'

'Authorities. Had to furnish a decent home for the boy or lose him. I couldn't stay settled then, with my wife gone. She was still so much a part of things, of our house, the streets, the places we used to go ... I went on the road, tried to forget. That kind of life was out of the question for a three-year-old. I had no choice. Either I bought a mechanical or I lost my son. I could find no one to take Jackie. Virgie's parents were dead and my own mother was in no position to raise a child. So I bought Margaret and, since we'd originally planned on a brother and sister for Jackie, I decided to go for the package deal. After all, I got 'em wholesale.'

'Hey!' The barman cocked an eyebrow. 'You're a mech salesman?'

'Until tomorrow. I'm quitting. My next job will be right here in L.A. and won't have a damn thing to do with mechanicals!' Producing his wallet, Rice handed the bartender a card. 'Read that.'

'Theodore A. Rice,' the beefy man pronounced carefully, 'Authorized representative for World Mechanicals.'

'No, no. The slogan at the bottom.'

'"A Dollar a Day Keeps Childbirth Away." So?'

Rice leaned forward, steely-eyed. 'So the damned fool who originated that ought to be roasted over a slow fire!'

'Just a slogan, Mac. Everybody knows it.'

'Exactly! Do you have any real conception of what that slogan and others like it have done to us?' Rice asked, a fresh whisky in his hand. 'Childbirth has been converted into a horror, a form of medieval torture in the minds of women today. For thirty bucks a month, any woman can have a bouncing baby made to order and delivered fresh-wrapped to her door. For less than it used to cost just to *feed* a human child, she can share the pleasures and joys of motherhood and avoid all the responsibilities.

'"Madam" I'd say, "don't risk your figure. Don't tie yourself down and miss all the fun. Get a mechanical! No baby sitters needed, no dirty diapers or squalling at three in the morning. No measles or mumps or tonsils out. Just a bonny little brat with a switch behind his ear. What'll it be, madam? A fat little bambino with dark eyes and an angel's smile, or a saucy-eyed little Irisher with freckles on her nose?

'"Or how's about you, fella? Tired of looking for the right girl? Want a ready made cutie who'll be one-hundred-percent yours? How did the old song go? 'I want a paper dolly I can call my own, a dolly other fellows cannot steal ...' Well, here she is, chum—a full-size babe with the old come-hither look reserved especially for you. Blonde? Brunette? Redhead? You name 'er, we've got 'er. Yours on easy payments!"'

Rice paused, breathing heavily, his glass empty.

The bartender, wise in the ways of his profession, maintained a listening silence.

'Ya know how this electronic illusion got started?' Rice demanded, tongue somewhat uncertain in his mouth, speech beginning to slur. 'Well, lemme tellya. People got lonesome. An' when somebody's old man died, 'long comes a mech to replace him. When a woman was sterile, she got her baby anyhow. When a Mr. Shy Guy wanted some female company, 'long comes a sponge rubber job right outa th' pinup mags. Jus' a few at first, here an' there, an' expensive as hell. But pretty soon the good ole American commercial know-how takes over and competition gets rough. Prices go down. A lotta people stop havin' babies. In nothin' flat, everybody is buyin' mechanicals ... you ... 'n ... me 'n everybody ...'

'Hate ta spoil your fun, Mac, but you're really loadin' one on. I'd ease up on them straight shots.'

'An' you know what th' trashdy is?' Rice continued over a filled glass, ignoring the advice. 'Th' trashdy is, we're all dyin' an' nobody cares! Pretty soon you 'n me will be in the same league with the goddamn ole water buffalo an' the dodo bird. Th' trashdy is that everybody is dyin' in a century designed for easy livin'. Say! Lesh drink a toast to th' joy of livin".'

The bartender extended a cautioning hand. 'No foolin', Mac, if I was you— Lookout! You're gonna ...'

Rice felt the room tip, rock crazily for no apparent reason. Faintly he heard the bartender's shout of warning, saw his face receding like a toy balloon down the length of an immense corridor which ended abruptly in a high fountaining of coloured lights.

Margaret was her usual cheery self when Rice finally switched her on.

'Morning, Ted darling.' She bussed him on the cheek. 'Sleep well?'

'This is July tenth,' he replied sullenly, nursing the remnants of a colossal hangover.

'Goodness! Have I been off that long? Honestly, Ted! I'll never get the housework done if you continue to leave me off for days at a time. How are the children?'

'Fine. Still sleeping.'

'If this is the tenth, then you've had your . . . your—'

' "Toot" is the word. And I feel lousy.'

'What's that cut above your eye? Did someone hit you?'

'My assailant was the floor of the Third Avenue Bar. I came off second best.'

She was instantly solicitous. 'You could have a concussion!'

'I'm fine.'

'You're angry again.'

'I'm fine and I'm not angry. Now, go wind the dog while I wake the kids.'

If only she would react, thought Rice, watching her silent withdrawal. If only *once* she would stomp her feet, throw things, scream at him. But always, always this everlasting indulgence! The spark which ignites a marriage, makes it glow, was missing. In love, he knew, there is violence; but Margaret's love was a calm, manufactured emotion which left him unsatisfied and edgy, a love unreal, intolerable. When he and Virgie had quarrelled, had things out and reconciled, they were actually much closer to one another for having weathered a personal storm. But with Margaret, the case was different.

Rice thought of the latest incident, two nights ago, when he had been with Skipper encouraging the dog to beg for a plastobone. Skipper was outdated, as modern dogs go, but he represented a link with the fading past which Margaret seemed bent on severing. She renewed the familiar subject of his purchasing a modernized electronic canine to replace the shaggy wind-up model, and he gave in to deep rage, thundering at her, gesturing, swearing. But she had remained impassive, turning aside his anger with her calm smile. Then, savagely, he had switched her off, as one might extinguish a glaring light. How frozen she had stood! How instantly drained of personality and movement! In that moment, facing her perfect, motionless body, he experienced the recurrent sense of guilt which invariably accompanied such action—as though he had taken a life, had murdered. Damning his own weakness, he had left her there, smiling, in the silent room.

'Daddy, Daddy, Daddy,' squealed Timmy after he was activated. 'Hooray, hooray, it's Picnic-Day! Hooray, hooray, it's Picnic-Day!'

'Hooray, hooray,' Rice repeated without enthusiasm, envisioning a hectic afternoon of child noise and forced amusement.

'Now quiet down. Your father's not feeling well,' Margaret cautioned from the hall, as Timmy zoomed and swooshed about the house playing Rocket.

Little Susan's enthusiasm matched that of her mechanical brother. She hopped around the living room, circling Rice, screaming out her delight in a voice that pierced his head like a driven needle.

'For the love of heaven, STOP!' he shouted at the whirling children, 'or I'll switch you both off!'

Under his stern threat, they quieted.

Margaret returned with Skipper. The dog had run down the previous evening chasing the electronic cat next door. He scampered rustily across the floor, high falsetto bark betraying the damaging effect of morning precipitation.

'Good ole Skip ... You need some oil, fella,' Rice told him, tickling his ears. 'Have you fixed in a jiff. Timmy, get the oilcan from the shelf.'

Rice was in the act of administering the proper lubricant when Jackie emerged from the hallway, rubbing sleep from his eyes.

'Hi, Mom. Hi, Dad. Morning everybody.' He yawned.

'Hi, scout,' Rice greeted him, roughing his already thoroughly tousled hair. 'Have a good rest?'

'Sure. Hey, this is Picnic-Day, isn't it? When are we leaving?'

'Soon as little sleepyheads like you get out of their pyjamas and into some breakfast.' He playfully swatted Jackie's bottom. 'Now git.'

Margaret took the boy's hand. 'Come on, dear. I have breakfast on the table.' And over her shoulder to Rice: 'I *do* think we should get an early start.'

Susan and Timmy bounded into the yard with Skipper, leaving Rice alone with his thoughts.

He said 'Hi, Mom' first, before 'Hi, Dad.' And the look in his eyes when she took his hand! Jackie is too young to see Margaret as I see her; he can't realize that she can never really love him as he loves her. The longer she's here, the harder it will be for Jackie when the break comes. I mustn't put off telling Margaret any longer. I'll tell her today. Today.

The bullet-car flowed soundlessly over the highway, blurring the trees, rushing the houses past, but to Rice the speed was illusion, strange trickery. His impatient mind, reaching for the moment when he would be alone with Margaret and able to tell her what he *must* tell her, changed minutes to hours. Head back against the seat, eyes closed, he imagined the car in lazy slow-motion, wheels barely turning, each blade of roadside grass separate and available to the eye, if one chose to look.

The ride to the picnic ground seemed endless.

'I'm bushed,' he said to Margaret after the car had parked

itself. 'Let's skip the games today and just relax in the shade.'

'But, Ted, the children ...'

'... can play without us. I have something to say to you, something important.'

She hesitated, watching the activity on the playing courts. The children, three elves in their picnic jumpers, fidgeted, desperately anxious to join the games, their eyes darting like imprisoned minnows in small white pools.

'In order to be enjoyed to the fullest, the games require *family* participation.'

'Nonsense.'

'Young and old, Ted. The games ...'

'To hell with the games!' he snapped. 'Are you going to listen to what I have to say or not?'

'Of course, darling. If you really *want* to talk ...' She smiled, pressed his hand. 'The children can join the Hartleys.' She pointed across the wide picnic lawn to a group of rioting players engaged in a vigorous game of Magneball. 'Run along, you three. And be careful.'

'Wheeeeeeee!' pealed little Susan and, hands linked, the happily released trio sprang towards the courts.

'If we're going to talk, we can at least be comfortable,' Margaret said, unpacking a blanket and spreading it over the prickling grass.

Every gesture perfect, thought Rice, watching her hands. Every movement graceful and sure. She's so alive, so amazingly human, possessing such vibrancy and warmth, that sometimes even I find it difficult to think of her as artificially created of wire and circuit and cog. Certainly Jackie has come to love her. She's good and kind and smiles a great deal. These things matter to Jackie. The fact that she isn't human does not matter. Not at all. The situation, therefore, is grave.

'What are you thinking about, Ted?' Her blue eyes were steady on his.

'About you. About how beautiful you are.' He plucked a single dandelion from the grass and held its orange-gold face, like a miniature sun, in the cupped palm of his hand. 'This is a weed masquerading as a flower. Beautiful, possessing many virtues, but actually a weed which must be removed before its deep tap root smothers the surrounding grass. Unless it is, there will eventually be room only for the dandelion.'

'What has all this . . .'

'You're like the dandelion, Margaret. You're smothering Jackie's love. He has grown to love you far more than he does me. Up to now, I've been just a visiting relative who comes home from some distant place to spend Christmas and summer vacations with you. When he was younger, he cried whenever I shut you off, as though I had beaten him. Even now he watches me lose my temper, swear, bang the furniture, and I see him looking at me, and I know he's comparing us, weighing us. The scales are in your favour. I'm home to stay now, and as long as you're here, he'll always be comparing. I can't, I won't, compete with a mechanical for my son's affection!'

She sucked in her breath, sharply. He could see that his words had struck with the force of hurled stones.

'Have you thought this all out, Ted? Isn't there some *other* way?' She was actually trembling. 'You know how much I love you.'

'You only *think* you love me, Margaret. What you mistake for love is only conditioning. Receptors can be re-fed, patterned responses erased, new ones substituted. At Central Exchange they'll alter you, Margaret. You'll never know I existed.'

'Ted, you can't!'

'There's no other way.'

A silence between them.

Despite himself, Rice again experienced a twinge of guilt. Perhaps he had broken the news in too ruthless a fashion. But it was imperative that she understand his position, and he had considered it impossible to pierce her shell of calm. That she would be visibly shaken by his words was totally unexpected. Of course, he reasoned, no mechanical likes the idea of complete reorientation. On these grounds, her behaviour seemed less surprising. But still ...

'Why have you told me all this?' she asked him. 'Why didn't you turn me in suddenly, without my knowing in advance? I'd have preferred that.' Her hands moved nervously on her skirt, toyed with the locket at her neck, now touched at her hair like two restless birds unable to fly away from her body.

'Because I need your help. Jackie mustn't know the truth ... not now. Later, when he's older, better able to evaluate facts for himself, he'll understand. I'll tell him something about your having to go on a long trip for reasons of health. He'll believe me if you'll back me up. Will you?'

'If that's what you want,' she replied softly, head down, her fingers turning and turning the dandelion he had discarded. 'I'll do anything you want, Ted ... because I love you.'

'Timmy and Susan can stay with Jackie for a while,' he hurried on, 'to make your leaving easier for him. In time, he'll adjust.'

'Yes ... he'll adjust.'

The drowsy rustle of leaves in summer air. The distant hum of voices from the playing courts.

'Well, then, it's settled.'

'All settled. You'd better call the children in for lunch.'

After lunch, Rice gambolled in the scented grass with the whooping children, imitating, to their vast delight, a bear, a gorilla, a whale, a jet train, and a moon rocket. He ran races with them and organized a rodeo, in which he doubled in brass as a fiercely snorting brahma bull and a bucking bronc.

On the way home, they sang folk songs, and watched the sun go down over the ocean. The day, everyone agreed, had been a huge success.

But, that night, Rice could not sleep.

The headboard whispered, '3 a.m., sir,' when he questioned the hour. He lay on his back, hands laced behind his head, staring into the ghostly darkness of the room. In the moon-painted sky, a copter whirred past like a giant night insect seeking distant city lights, and Rice thought of Virginia. In recent weeks, he had been finding it remarkably difficult to remember many of the things about her that he wished to remember; time had hidden her image as a coin is hidden in deep waters.

The drone of the copter faded into Margaret's quiet breathing from the bed beside his and now *her* face drifted into his mind, superimposed over the dim reflection of Virginia. He saw, in infinite detail, each curling black hair of her downswept lashes, long and trembling against the rose of her cheek. He saw her quivering lips form words, four startling words of the afternoon: '*... because I love you.*'

Impossible, that a mechanical could love as Virginia had loved; that a being of metal and glass—of wires, however cunningly woven—could fathom and experience such deeply genuine emotion.

Yet was it conceivable, Rice wondered in the pressing darkness, that somehow an unknown process had taken place in Margaret—that far back in the green cave of her brain, among the delicate spiderwebbing of silver wires and hidden circuits, an emotion had come into being above and beyond that of the purely mechanical?

Rice relived his initial shock of the afternoon, when, in direct vocal assault, he had unexpectedly found a chink in her armour, when he had all but moved her to tears—ridiculous in itself, for a mechanical cannot cry! But now, despite his earlier rationalization of her strange behaviour, he was puzzled, vaguely disturbed.

At seven, a robin's sweet song awoke him. He felt a breath of air against his closed eyes from the passing fluttering of small wings. Burying his head deeper in the snow-soft pillow, he tried to ignore the insistent twitterings. However, he knew the damn thing would begin a banshee shrieking if he didn't get out of bed. Irritably, he staggered into his slippers, and the robin settled with feathered grace upon his outstretched hand. Rice flipped the body-switch and placed the immobilized alarm bird on the night stand.

He dressed before waking Margaret.

'I've had breakfast,' he lied to her when she asked. Today he wasn't hungry.

She nibbled toast and drank orange juice in silence. He avoided her eyes, finding inconsequential kitchen duties to occupy his hands while she ate. After half-finishing her food, she said, her voice very distinct in the morning room, 'I guess it's time.'

'Early yet,' he said, not meeting her eyes. 'No hurry at all. They open the doors at eight-thirty. We can set the car for a slow drive.'

A silence.

'Did you ... tell the children good-bye?' he asked.

'Last night. We won't need to wake them. They'll be fine until you get back.' She put on black gloves, carefully fitting each finger, pulling them tight.

'Margaret, I'm sorry. Honest to God, I'm sorry it has to be this way.'

'Don't say anything else, Ted. Just let's go.'

'All right,' he said. 'Let's go.'

A brief shower had cleansed the sky and the morning was fresh and clear. The trees, their leaves pendant with rain jewels, glittered in the warming sunlight.

Through the open car window Rice inhaled the rich after-scent of rain, and sighed. He wished it had not turned out to be such a damned fine day. The sky outside should have been grey, the trees stark and cold, like mourners along the street, as the car, a silver coffin, passed them by.

He tried to think of something to say to Margaret as the bullet-car bore them steadily through the crystal morning towards the massive white stone building which housed Central Exchange. He tried to think of words which would not sound wrong the moment they were uttered. But he found none and remained silent.

It was she who turned to him in the moving car and

spoke first. 'Ted, what are you doing?' Her voice was strange.

'Doing?' he echoed, facing her.

'To me, to Jackie, to yourself.'

'Margaret, you're not going to question me *now*? We've gone over this, the reasons for my decision, the factors involved. Surely you must realize—'

'Damn your reasons!' she exploded, eyes blazing at him, gloved hands clenched. 'Are they fair? Do they take *my* feelings into consideration? Do they, Ted? Answer me! Do they?'

He couldn't answer her. A door was opening somewhere deep inside him and light was miraculously flooding in to illuminate a room he had never allowed himself to enter. He was blind, and her words were sight.

'I'm a mechanical, isn't that the answer, Ted? A bloodless machine that can be switched off at will, ignored, cursed, shouted at, and destroyed, a creature without emotion, without feeling. Well, you're wrong, Ted. So very wrong. Men built me, gave me human impulses, human desires, put into me a part of themselves, a part of their own humanity. I feel hunger and thirst and cold and pain. But more, Ted! I feel a *human* hunger, a *human* thirst, a desire to be respected for myself, as an individual, as I respect others, a desire to be loved as I love others. Can't you see how wrong you've been? I've held all of these things within because I was taught enduring humility and consummate patience by those who fashioned me. I was taught to behave rationally and calmly, to accept, to always accept and never question or rebel. But now it's ended, and I've lost ... You've rejected me, Ted, and I wasn't prepared for this ... I can't accept this, but I don't know *how* to fight. I only know I must, and I don't know how.'

Her lips were trembling, her whole body swaying in the tide of released rage and sorrow.

'Lord, Lord, Margaret ...' He placed a gentle hand beneath her chin and lifted her bowed head slowly. 'You're *crying*!'

Rice stopped the car and took her, trembling, into his arms, saying her name over and over, quietly, trembling himself, and softly, tenderly, he kissed her.

Then, setting the controls at manual he turned the car around and, with one arm holding her close on the seat beside him, he drove carefully home through the warm summer streets, knowing that never again—never ever again, in all the years to come—would he switch her off.

THE END

LOGAN'S WORLD *by* WILLIAM F. NOLAN

Doomsday plus ten years—and Earth is still a living horror. The last battle burned the planet to a charred husk, leaving only a few scattered tribes struggling desperately to survive . . . like the corps of elite killers who served the old dictatorship . . . or the sadistic bands of motorcyle hoods, prowling the ruins for victims . . . or the slavers, mutants and madmen preying on those who still hoped to rebuild the future . . . and a brave few like Logan and his family—the hunted refugees in a world of vicious predators.

This is LOGAN'S WORLD

0 552 10734 4—**70p**

DRAGONSINGER *by* ANNE McCAFFREY

When Mellony, daughter of Yanas Sea Holder, arrived at the Harper Craft Hall, she came in style, aboard a bronze dragon followed by her nine fire lizards. The Masterharper of Pern aware of her unique skills, had chosen her as his only girl apprentice. But the holdless girl had first to overcome many heartaches in this strange new life. Two things sustained her; her devoted lizards—a subject on which she was fitted to instruct her Masters—and the music . . . music of transcendent beauty, music—making where at last she was accepted. In the Great Hall, Menolly could fulfill her destiny.

0 552 10881 2—**85p**